THE CROW BROTHERS COLLECTION

Old West Romances

KRISTY MCCAFFREY

The Crow and The Coyote

In Arizona Territory, Hannah Dobbin travels through Cañon de Chelly, home to the Navajo, in search of a sorcerer who murdered her pa. Only when she retrieves the silver cross taken from her father's corpse will she be able to free her pa's spirit and allow him to be at peace.

Bounty hunter Jack Boggs—known as The Crow—is on the trail of a vile Mexican bandito when he discovers Hannah and her companion, a superstitious old Navajo woman. He knows he must protect them, but with the shadows of Hallowtide descending, more dark magic is at hand than any of them know.

The Crow and The Bear

Bounty hunter Callum Boggs—sometimes called The Crow—arrives in the mining town of Silverton on a cold October day in search of a man who has committed unspeakable crimes. Skilled in the technique of dream scouting, Cal has narrowed the location of the criminal to Silas Ravine. No normal man would dare to venture into this region, where so many gruesome and unexplained murders have taken place —a piece of land forever haunted where Death still walks. But Boggs is no normal man...

Jennie Livingstone knows her papa is in trouble. When none of the local men will come to her aid, she must accept a newly-arrived stranger—a half-Comanche bounty hunter—as her only ally. As they head into the mountains to track Jennie's father, she can hear more than the whispers of man. The mines carry spirits, and her only hope in navigating the living and the dead lies with The Crow.

But is Jennie prepared for the consequences of where her fate with Callum Boggs may lead? And is she the woman who can hold fast to

The Crow's heart after all his years alone? Bewitched by the beautiful young woman, Callum must do everything he can to stay one step ahead of the spirits that can't rest—just to keep Jennie and himself alive.

A Murder of Crows

Bounty hunter Kester "Kit" Boggs, along with his brothers, tracks and destroys the vilest of men, both from this world and the next. With a Scottish and Comanche lineage, his connection to the supernatural is tied directly to the crow. For too long, he's been hunting *El Viejo del Saco*, a demon known as The Bag Man who feeds on the blood of children. A rumor leads Kit to the Mexican frontier, where he must find a man called Hamish Kerr. But with Hallowtide descending, Kit has lost his ability to hear spirits, and his only hope is a woman whose family is a sworn enemy to the Boggs' clan.

Eliza McCulloch's ancestors hail from Scotland, her clan carrying an ancient curse and a warning—a McCulloch may never bind herself to a Boggs. When Eliza learns that Hamish Kerr stole her family's book of spells, the McCulloch Grimoire, nearly two decades ago, she sets out to reclaim it. Often called witch, she possesses a unique skill to open doorways to the other side. But when she finds herself beholden to a Boggs for protection, her abilities take an unexpected turn.

As Kit and Eliza unearth far more than a stolen book, they must work together if they are to survive. But with the past pushing into their future, can they resist the growing desire between them? Is it possible for a Boggs and a McCulloch to find lasting love? Or will defeating the demon separate them forever?

The Crow and The Coyote

First edition published by Prairie Rose Publications, 2014.

The Crow and The Bear

First edition published by Prairie Rose Publications, 2015.

A Murder of Crows

First edition published by Prairie Rose Publications, 2018.

The Crow Brothers Collection

Copyright © 2021 *K. McCaffrey LLC*

Cover Design: earthlycharms.com

Editor First Editions: Cheryl Pierson

Author Photo property of K. McCaffrey LLC

E-book ISBN-13: 978-1-952801-14-3

Print ISBN-13: 978-1-952801-15-0

kmccaffrey.com
kristy@kmccaffrey.com

OTHER BOOKS BY KRISTY MCCAFFREY

Historical Western Romance

The Wren

The Dove

The Sparrow

The Blackbird

The Bluebird

The Songbird (Novella)

Echo of the Plains (Wings Short Story)

The Starling

The Canary

The Nighthawk

The Swan

The Falcon

Into The Land Of Shadows

The West: A Romance Collection

Rosemary

Alice: Bride of Rhode Island

Contemporary Western Romance

Blue Sage

The Peppermint Tree

A Mirthful Wish

PRAISE FOR THE CROW SERIES

"With just the right amount of mystic and adventure …"
~ Michelle Reed, Sunshine Lake Reviews

"A suspenseful ride into the supernatural with a western twist."
~ Devon McKay, author of *Lead Me Into Temptation*, Gold Dust Bride
Series

THE CROW AND THE COYOTE

Among the red-rock canyons of the Navajo, bounty hunter Jack Boggs
—known as The Crow—aids Hannah Dobbin in a quest to save her
pa's soul during Hallowtide.

CHAPTER ONE

Cañon de Chelly, Arizona Territory
October 1877

J ack Boggs came upon the camp in the blackness of night. A form lay near a smoldering fire. A quick perusal told him it was female. Disappointed, he rested his gun against his thigh from where he crouched.

He'd followed these tracks all day, but instead of leading him to Ignacio Lopez, they ended here. He had no interest in befriending anyone, but perhaps the woman might have seen Lopez in the area.

The end of a barrel jammed hard between his shoulder blades. "Do not move."

Shocked by the sound of a gravelly, Indian-inflected voice, he couldn't believe a woman had crept up on him.

He let the Colt slide to the ground before him, then slowly raised his arms.

"Stand, and move away from that gun," she said.

Hopefully, she wouldn't notice the second one still holstered. He stood. The metal dug into his back again—from the feel of it, likely a double-barreled shotgun—prompting him forward. He stepped over his weapon, and heard the Indian woman retrieve it.

"Hannah, wake up," the woman said as they approached.

Jack chanced a glance over his shoulder. A short, elderly Navajo woman eyed him with suspicion.

The female on the ground stirred, then sprang to her feet.

With a gasp, her hand came to her chest. "Oh, my word, Sani."

Forced closer by the persistent Sani, he could see Hannah's disheveled dark hair framed a youthful complexion.

"I told you we were followed," the old woman said.

Hannah's gaze shifted to him. "Who are you, sir?"

"The name's Jack. I'm in pursuit of bounty." He ceased inching forward, and the shotgun dug into his back once again.

"What bounty would that be?"

"A bandito by the name of Ignacio Lopez. I mean no harm to you and soft shoes back there." He nodded over his shoulder.

Hannah considered him, then agreed. "Sani, put the gun down."

To Jack's surprise, the Indian woman acquiesced. Carefully, he lowered his arms. "Would either of you by chance know anything about Lopez?"

Sani came to stand beside Hannah, gripping the shotgun in one hand and his weapon in the other. Even in the dark, he sensed her brittle glare.

"We might," Hannah answered. "Would you care to join us at our fire?" She scanned behind her. "At what is *left* of our fire?" she amended.

He gave a curt nod. "Might I trouble you for the return of my gun?"

Hannah motioned for Sani to give it back, which the old woman did, her features schooled in a skeptical frown.

He wasted no time holstering the weapon, hoping to gain their trust.

They all settled around the barely glowing embers.

Hannah stoked the fire, re-igniting a small blaze, then spoke in soft undertones to Sani. Jack caught snippets of Spanish mixed with a dialect he assumed to be Navajo. He knew only a smattering, the

Navajo language far more complex than any he'd encountered in the past few years of hunting bounties in Texas and the territories.

Hannah turned her gaze upon him, now viewing him as sternly as old Sani. After a moment of contemplation, she murmured again to the Navajo woman.

"It's rude to talk behind someone's back," he said, removing his hat and running fingers through shoulder-length hair.

"I agree," Hannah replied. "Are you called Crow?"

Even in the darkness, his jet-black hair was hard to miss. That had to account for why she guessed the moniker frequently attributed to him.

"Yes," he replied.

Hannah took a deep breath. "Well, then, Sani and I would ask for your assistance—in exchange, of course—for our help in locating *Señor* Lopez."

"You know his whereabouts?"

She nodded, but then amended, "Well, maybe not his location *precisely*, but we've some idea who he might be with."

"And who's that?"

She regarded him in silence. For such a young and pretty thing, she was turning out to be a shrewd negotiator. "Do we have a deal?"

"I've no idea what you're asking me to do."

"You tell him," Sani said.

"We're after a Navajo called Hastin Yazhe." Hannah spoke quietly. "He has something I want returned, a silver cross that belonged to my pa. If the man you trail is in these canyons, Yazhe will get him—if not now, then eventually."

Pinpricks pierced the back of Jack's neck, bringing his attention fully to the young woman across from him.

"Who is this Yazhe?" he asked.

"A sorcerer. A demon. Depends on your religious leanings, I suppose. I believe him to practice evil."

"Why would you come after him alone? Are there no men aiding you? Where are your husbands?"

"I've no husband," Hannah replied, "and Sani has long been

without her love. I wouldn't pursue this man if it wasn't of utmost importance."

"And why is that?"

"He murdered my pa and left his spirit in limbo. When I get that cross back, I'll be able to undo the dark works that have imprisoned my pa's soul. I'll be able to set him free."

A foreboding of apprehension caught Jack by surprise, sending a shiver down his spine. He knew something of spirits and superstitions, but he also knew that men begat violence for no other reason than that they could.

He also knew that the two women before him, while spouting paranoia, were entirely lucid—and deadly serious.

That concerned him most of all.

HANNAH AWOKE BEFORE DAWN FROM HER PALLET BY THE TINY FIRE SHE and Sani had allowed themselves. For the first time since her pa died some three weeks ago, her dreams had been calm. She turned on her side and watched the man called Crow, slumbering several feet away beside a horse he'd retrieved the previous night. The presence of both had kept the spooks at bay, and a feeling of safety washed over her.

She wondered if trusting the man was wise, but Sani grudgingly accepted him. Truthfully, they could use his help. None of the Navajo men would accompany them—they insisted on distancing themselves from the actions of *two women not in their right minds*.

Hannah knew the beliefs of the Navajo—that stirring up spirits would not end well—but she had no choice, not if she wanted to help her pa. She knew, however, that if she and Sani weren't careful, they could both end up dead.

Mister Crow consumed a large space in this world with his obvious physical presence, and a look in his dark eyes that was both remote and calculating. She sensed he walked a fine line between justice and violence. It didn't frighten her, but she did wonder if she could trust him.

He awoke, stood, and immediately checked his horse. Then, he looked directly at her.

"Mornin'," he said.

Hannah pushed to a sitting position and nodded. Sani snored softly beside her.

Mister Crow produced a bag of grain and fed his animal.

"Did you walk?" he asked.

"No. Our animals are up that way." She indicated the direction with a nod.

"You're on the trail of an evil Navajo, as well as likely following Lopez—just as evil, I might add—and yet you let your animals run free *and* you had a fire last night." He shook his head, his black hair brushing the edge of his shirt. "You're not doing a good job of hiding yourself."

Hannah stood and moved toward him, to not disturb Sani with their voices. "We're not close to those we follow."

He stepped back from his horse and scanned their surroundings, then planted hands on hips and fixed her again with that penetrating gaze. "How do you know?"

Hannah watched him, liking the way his eyes slanted slightly down, and the stubble that covered his face, tanned from the sun. His hair was so black—like an Indian—but he didn't have the look of the Navajo, or the Hopi, or any of the peoples in the area she and her pa had visited.

"Sani has visions," she replied.

His mouth turned up in the barest hint of a smile. "Naturally."

"So, your name is Jack Crow?"

"No. It's Jack *Boggs*. I've been called Crow from time to time."

"Are you Indian?"

He ignored her question. "How did you come to be here, Hannah ..." He gave her a questioning look.

"Dobbin. I told you, I'm chasing Hastin Yazhe."

"No. How did you come to be in the territory?"

"Oh." She glanced at Sani, likely the only friend she had. "I came with my pa, Dr. Walter Dobbin, three years ago from Ohio."

"He was a doctor?"

"No, not like that. He had a Doctorate in Anthropology. We came to study the Indians in the area. It's called ethnography. For the last year, we traveled among the Navajo, recording their culture, their customs, their language ... just about everything. He planned to write a book about it."

"Why was he killed?"

"While the Navajo are generally a peaceful people, not all were happy about our work, viewing it as an intrusion. Yazhe was a dissenter, among other things. When he killed my pa, he took the cross. I want it, and I mean to get it back."

"How do you know he has it?"

Hannah glanced down at the toe of her boot, scuffed and dirty. "A dream." She lifted her eyes to his, silently challenging him to laugh in her face, or shake his head and walk away.

Instead, he watched her.

Hannah's pulse quickened. There'd been men—both white and Indian—that had displayed interest in her. Every single one paled in comparison to Jack Boggs.

The barest hint of a smile once again graced his mouth, briefly distracting Hannah.

"You're not the type to explain yourself, are you?" he asked.

"Would you believe me if I did?"

"Trailing these men isn't safe. What you ought to do is head home. If Lopez is with Yazhe, then I'll do my best to retrieve your cross."

"No. But I do appreciate the offer."

Sani began to stir. Hannah turned from Mister Boggs and headed toward where she thought the horse and mule had gone off to.

JACK CHECKED HIS SADDLE, BUT IT WAS JUST A COVER SO HE COULD WATCH Hannah Dobbin walk away. She had the damnedest eyes, a gray-green that reminded him of the sagebrush that grew in the endless red desert in this area. She was direct in a way that most women weren't, and it cast a spell on him.

Did she speak the truth? Was she really after a family memento? Or, maybe she was a decoy, tied to Lopez in some way. Even, perhaps, the man's woman.

The thought angered him when it shouldn't have. When did he care about the women Lopez bedded?

"She is good." Sani's voice startled him, as did her sudden proximity. That was the second time she'd sneaked up on him.

"Pardon?"

Sani brought her gnarled hand to his, grasping tightly. His appeared that much larger, entwined with her smaller one.

"I hope you're not making a play for me old lady," he said. "I'm afraid you're not my type."

She glanced at the direction Hannah had recently trod. "She is."

"I never thought I'd find nosy biddies this far west."

Sani narrowed her eyes at him. "Hannah cannot live with the Diné forever. Her *padre* is gone. When this is done, you shall take her."

The elderly woman released his hand and returned to the gear piled near the ashes of the campfire.

Jack felt the finality of her words as if it were a prophecy.

CHAPTER TWO

J ack soon realized that the horse and the mule the two women
utilized were old and slow. Hannah walked—her steps kicking
red dust that coated her brown skirt—while Sani rode the gray-
brown gelding, and the mule carried their gear.

Jack brought his mount to Hannah and reached for the reins she
held.

"Climb up," he said.

She inclined her head back and squinted up at him. "I can walk."

"At this pace, we'd be lucky to catch a turtle."

He extended his arm. She grasped it, and he hauled her behind
him. He liked the feel of strength in her grip. She was no will-o'-the-
wisp. Taking the reins of Sani's horse, he used his mount to increase
the pace.

By mid-afternoon, they came to the remains of a settlement.

"No." Hannah's voice broke, and she slid from his horse and hit the
ground running.

He pulled one of his Colt revolvers, dismounted, and performed a
swift inspection of the area.

Hannah rushed to the bodies of two Navajo, a man and a
woman, lying in a heap beside a collapsed hogan. She frantically
inspected them for signs of life. Shaking her head back and forth,

she stifled a sob, then turned and ran to a child's body several feet away.

Jack continued to keep a keen eye on the surroundings, in the event the perpetrator remained in the vicinity. He noticed that Sani had dismounted but didn't approach the dead bodies.

Hannah stood and swung around. "Why Sani? Why would he do this?" Anguish held her body rigid.

The Navajo woman didn't speak.

"Who?" Jack asked.

"Hastin." Hannah all but spit the word from her mouth.

"Why would a Navajo kill other Navajo?" he asked.

"We must not handle the bodies," Sani said, her voice wooden and flat.

"Bullshit!" Hannah screamed. "I will not tiptoe around while Hastin commits these awful crimes. And I surely won't abandon them —" Her voice caught, and she faltered. "Because of your belief that they will haunt us." Tears rolled down her cheeks. "We must bury them," she whispered. Her gaze shifted to him. "We mustn't leave them to the vultures."

Unnerved by her outburst, Jack holstered his weapon and went to her. He wanted to offer comfort but restrained himself from touching her. They hardly knew one another, and it was improper, but the truth was, he didn't want to risk her spurning him. Something in him didn't want Hannah to shy away before he had a chance to know her better.

"We'll do our best for these people," he said. "If it's any consolation, this may not have been done by Hastin. This has all the markings of Lopez." *The gunshot to the child's head ...*

Her sage-green eyes met his. "Then we both pursue men who violate the natural order of life."

Jack silently agreed.

EXHAUSTED, HANNAH NEVERTHELESS WORKED TO PREPARE A MEAL FOR Mister Boggs now that nightfall was upon them. He'd helped her all afternoon in burying the bodies of the Navajo they found, and she was immensely grateful. Sani had disappeared, as was her way. Hannah loved the old woman, but there were times when she tested the limits of that affection.

Mister Boggs appeared and sat beside her.

"Where's Sani?" he asked.

"She'll return, in time," Hannah replied. "To be around the dead fills the Navajo with great paranoia. I fear that if I die, she'd leave me to the birds and beetles."

"Not if I have anything to say. I'll take care of you, Hannah."

After such a macabre day, with grief pressing heavy on her, she was struck by the humor in his statement. "I've never had a man make an offer to watch over my corpse, Mister Boggs."

"Then, I'm happy to be the first. And you should call me Jack."

She glanced at him. "I think I'll call you Crow. It suits you."

"Then it's *Mister* Crow to you."

She made a noncommittal sound. "You must be hungry. I've made boiled corn and squash, and flour cakes. And coffee."

She handed a plate filled with food to him, and a tin cup with the hot liquid.

"My thanks," he said.

"I owe you for today."

"Did you know them?" he asked around mouthfuls of food.

"Not well, but my pa had spent some time in this area, visiting with the people. Their names were Naalnish and Shadi, and the child was Mosi." Such a terrible thing, adding additional weight to the loss of her pa.

She shifted to gain a better view of the man beside her, sipping at her coffee. "Where are you from, Mister Crow?"

"I hail from Missouri, but these days, I like the territories."

"Have you been a bounty hunter for long?"

"I spent some time as a Texas Ranger. Now, I follow leads I hear about through the grapevine."

"A Ranger grapevine?"

"Something like that." He set his empty plate aside.

"If you catch men like this Lopez you've described," she said, "then you do an important job."

"I hope so. Can't abide what some men think they can get away with."

"My pa believed in the good of others." Her eyes met Jack's. "But I know that, in some, there *is* no good. I expect you know that, too."

"I do, Hannah."

The sound of her name sounded familiar and intimate, sending a shiver down her spine.

Where had he come from, this man who appeared in the dark?

"Are you a ghost?" she asked.

His intriguing mouth cracked a partial smile. "This place does make you wonder, doesn't it?" His attention shifted above her shoulder. "Don't move."

She sensed the animal behind her, although she wondered more about the man before her. Mysterious and compelling, was he any different from the *criaturas* that inhabited the wild places?

"It's alright, Crow." She glanced over her shoulder at the coyote standing beyond in the shadows. "He's a friend."

CHAPTER THREE

J ack watched as Hannah scooted toward the coyote, crooning and extending her hand to the animal. Its gaze settled mostly on Jack. Finally, though, it crouched and approached Hannah, residing beside her.

"I call him Hok'ee," she said, stroking the beast's neck.

"Is he your pet?"

"No. He's only been with us since we began this journey."

"I've never known a coyote to willingly mingle with humans."

"This one is different," she said quietly.

"In what way?"

The animal lay down and placed his head on Hannah's lap, eyes still upon Jack. Jack's gaze drifted to the woman, serene and strong. He liked the color of her hair—a deep burgundy captured in a braid— and thought it would look lovely spread across her shoulders, covering the soft complexion of her creamy skin. She wore a duster that had seen better days, but he'd caught glimpses of her fine figure, despite it.

"You'll probably snicker when I say," she said, "but I'll say it anyway. Some of my pa's spirit is in Hok'ee. All the more reason to retrieve his cross and set him free."

Distracted by his thoughts of the woman beside him, he didn't register her admission at first. He frowned. "Shapeshifter?"

"No. Not the same thing."

"Why do you believe the coyote is possessed of your father's spirit?"

"Just a feeling. But I've not told Sani, so please don't say anything to her."

"Why?"

Hannah rubbed her forehead, clearly fatigued. "If she knew, she'd want nothing to do with Hok'ee. The Navajo consider it a misfortune to interact with the dead in any way, but I don't agree with this belief."

"You should get some rest. I'll keep an eye out for Sani."

She nodded and spread her bedroll beside the fire. A chill settled in the late October night. Jack tugged his long coat against him, then retrieved a blanket from his gear. He brought it to Hannah and covered her, despite the sheepskin blanket she already possessed. Hok'ee watched intently from his spot curled against her.

Lucky scoundrel.

Startled, Hannah protested. "No, you need it," she said.

"You can return it later." He allowed himself the luxury of touching her a tad longer than necessary.

"Thank you."

Soon, she slept, and he fought the urge to lie down beside her. Something about Hannah Dobbin called to him, sparking a longing for connection, more than just the obvious physical yearning.

Hannah lived in a place between this world and the next, unafraid. Weary himself of chasing men who inflicted pain and suffering onto innocents, he felt a tangible pull to her, as if she were a clear stream flowing in a desert oasis and he was parched to his very soul.

What would it be like to love a woman like this, a woman filled with the life of the earth, the animals, and the sky above?

He never would've suspected he'd find such a woman in a remote area like this, walking among the Navajo as if one of them, chasing a madman in search of a relic that could save her pa's soul.

There was little doubt in his mind about what he would do next.

HANNAH AWOKE WITH A START AS THE SKY BEGAN TO LIGHTEN. SHE TRIED to shake the dread tingling in her limbs. The presence of her pa pressed close, and she knew he'd been in her dreams, but she couldn't recall the images; the memories slipped away like smoke in the wind.

Sani slept nearby, having returned during the night, but Hok'ee was gone. That wasn't unusual, however, for him.

A swift scan confirmed what Hannah suspected. Jack was gone, as well.

Perhaps he went to scout the perimeter, to keep them safe, but she wasn't fool enough to believe that.

He'd left them.

The disappointment cut sharp and deep, taking her by surprise.

Why did she care that he'd abandoned them? But he hadn't, not really. He had no obligation to her, no real reason to help except that maybe he wanted to. She'd offered aid in locating his fugitive, Lopez, but that had been a somewhat empty promise. She had no idea if Lopez was with Yazhe, but if she had to guess, the two would eventually cross paths.

She remembered the look in Jack's dark eyes, filled with justice and compassion. And perhaps amusement? Had he simply tolerated her until he could extricate himself from two *loco* females slowing down his hunt for a Mexican criminal?

She was certain his gaze had held a hint of ... something else, and it had sparked a place buried inside her. But she must've been wrong since he'd run off during the night without even a goodbye.

She stood and busied herself with camp chores. Soon, Sani awoke and accepted Jack's absence with little commentary. After Hannah packed the horse and mule, they were on their way heading farther into Cañon de Chelly, the sheer sandstone walls towering over them.

Sani knew this place intimately, had lived here during her childhood. She'd been on the Long Walk in '63 and returned in '68. She didn't like to talk of it, except that she'd lost Luis during that time. The

Navajo had taken him prisoner many years before, and Sani had grown to love him.

Hannah trusted Sani's visions. To her, the elderly Navajo woman remained tuned to her instincts in a way that few white men understood. Hannah didn't completely grasp it either, but after spending months living amongst indigenous peoples in the area, she felt her soul entwined with nature, her senses acutely aware of the blue sky, the red dirt, and the crisp wind.

Was this how it was with Crow? All day, her thoughts slipped back to him.

As if a compass, Sani led them into the canyon's interior, but there was no denying their slow progress. This seemed not to distress Sani, so Hannah let go any sense of urgency.

They watered the animals late in the afternoon at a perennial spring, so didn't stop until gray hues mired the sky.

Sani paced while Hannah removed knapsacks tied to the mule.

"What is it?" Hannah asked.

Sani stopped. "There is no voice here."

Gooseflesh arose on Hannah's arms. She pulled the shotgun resting against the horse's hide and cracked the barrel to check if it was loaded, then aimed it into the nothingness surrounding them.

Gusts blew icy air into her face, making her eyes water. Scrub brush shook, setting her on edge.

Someone is there.

"Stand behind me, Sani," she said in a low voice.

Back to back, they kept watch for the threat so palpable in the air. The high canyon walls loomed high, effectively boxing them in. The horse whinnied in agitation and Hannah's eyes darted back and forth, her hands chilled as they gripped the weapon tightly.

"What color is the wind, Sani?" Hannah whispered.

In defeat, Sani answered, "It is red."

Hannah readied for a fight. Red was a bad wind, believed to be placed by Coyote, the great Trickster. Every year, a red wind took the lives of Navajo children.

Where was Hok'ee? Sani would believe the animal to be foe, but

Hannah knew, in the marrow of her bones, that Hok'ee carried her pa's spirit in this place. It was the only way he'd been able to stay with them. Perhaps he sent the wind to help?

She'd never convince Sani to place trust in a coyote, but Hannah hoped for an otherworldly intervention, nonetheless.

The mule moved, bumping them, and agitation gripped the horse. Distracted, Hannah tried to move away but the animals blocked her view. The man came from nowhere. Stunned, Hannah held tight to the shotgun, but large hands wrested it from her. Screaming, she clawed at the assailant. A punch to the face sent her sprawling backward.

Panic jolted through her at the blast of gunfire.

Sani!

Scrambling to her feet, she launched herself at the large Mexican. He grabbed her by the neck, choking her and she clawed at his hands in desperation. His face contorted, framed by dark, greasy hair, and cold eyes filled with malevolence.

He meant to end her life. She fought, desperately, to make him stop but her lungs clawed for breath, frantic.

And then there was no more pain.

And no more struggle.

With no breath, her vision narrowed.

Then, she was gone.

CHAPTER FOUR

J ack slid from his horse with the animal still in motion and ran to Hannah. Sani's unmoving body lay just beyond, but he came to Hannah first.

Dropping to his knees, her ashen pallor punched him in the gut, and he knew she breathed no more.

No!

He wouldn't accept it. He left the women to protect them, not get them killed.

This can't happen!

Gently lifting Hannah's head with one hand and her torso with the other, he brought his mouth to hers and exhaled. Bringing her more fully into his arms, he elevated her and filled her lungs with air.

"Come back to me," he whispered, his voice ragged.

Carefully, he pushed her forward into a sitting position, then brought her back to recline, repeating this several times. He'd once seen a medicine man bring a man back in this manner. He continued to breathe into her.

"Hannah Dobbin, please come back to me."

Her body shuddered.

He pushed her upright as her lungs sucked in air, bracing himself behind her. Tenderly, he stroked her neck.

Still wheezing, she turned to him. "You came back."

"I'm sorry I left." Burying his hand into her hair, he kissed her cheek.

"Sani." Her voice broke, and she struggled to stand. He held her arm as she stumbled to the Navajo woman. They dropped on either side of Sani.

"She's been shot," Hannah said in a panic.

Jack pulled away bloodied clothing from Sani's shoulder. "Buckshot. She's been grazed. It's not bad."

"Is she alive?"

"Yes."

As they tended to Sani's wound, Jack asked, "Who was it?"

"A Mexican." Hannah's focus remained on extracting pellets from Sani's skin.

"Lopez." But how? Jack would've seen him slip past to get to the women. He stood. "I'll be back."

Hannah's head shot up. "What? You're leaving again?"

He knelt and brought a hand to her cheek. "No." He couldn't keep the emotion from his words. Hannah Dobbin had hold of him. "I'm just gonna check the area. You won't be out of my sight."

She nodded, not shying from his touch. "Be careful," she said.

In her gaze he saw tenderness. And need.

He made a fast perusal of the surroundings. In the dark it was difficult to see tracks, but as near as he could tell, Lopez had come upon the women from behind, possibly from a rocky outcropping. Maybe he'd been hiding there all along, and Jack had ridden right past him.

Why hadn't Lopez taken him out?

Nothing from Sani and Hannah had been stolen, not even their weapon. In fact, he was certain Sani had been shot by her own gun.

Further inspection revealed a smattering of confused prints and smears in the dirt.

Hok'ee?

Although Jack couldn't be certain, he had a strong feeling Lopez had fought with the coyote. Footprints led into the dark, but

Jack didn't dare follow. He wouldn't leave Hannah unprotected again.

But Lopez was likely not far, and possibly injured. Maybe fatally. Jack could only hope.

He returned to Hannah's side.

"No fire tonight," he said quietly, crouching beside her. "I don't suppose Sani could be moved?"

"Not far. Where is he?"

"I'm guessing he could be near."

"Are we safe here?"

Jack shook his head. "You haven't been safe since you entered this canyon. Will you let me escort you out?"

"No," Sani said, startling them both.

Hannah leaned close to the woman's face. "Thank goodness you're all right, Sani. Are you in any pain?"

"I will manage. We must find Hastin."

"I'll take both of you out of here," Jack said, "and then I'll find Hastin *and* Lopez. I give you my word."

Sani shook her head slightly. "You cannot do this without us."

Hannah turned to Jack. "We can help you, just as we originally agreed."

Helplessness hit Jack, an unaccustomed sensation. But Hannah Dobbin didn't belong to him, in any way; he had no say in her life. When this was over, if they made it out of here alive, he would have to change that.

"If that's what you wish, Hannah," he said.

"We'll watch over you, Crow," she said, the timbre of her voice reminding him of warm whiskey and steamy nights. "When I was dead, I saw it."

"What else did you see?"

Amusement filled her eyes. "I saw us." She glanced down, as an embarrassed smile briefly graced her mouth.

He watched her and grinned. Despite the danger they faced, hope started to grow in his heart that they'd make it out of this canyon in one piece.

CHAPTER FIVE

Hannah made Sani as comfortable as possible without any light. She gave her water to drink, and a flour cake that had been made that morning. Hannah also insisted on a bit of laudanum—she'd always carried some since her pa's aching joints had become more troublesome in the months before he was killed.

For the first time, thinking of him didn't squeeze her throat with grief and fill her chest with longing.

I saw him.

During her brief death—Jack insisted she couldn't have been gone long but refused to elaborate more when asked—she'd been with her pa. He was still close to this world, hovering near. He told her she'd been right about Hok'ee, that there were times when he could share the coyote's spirit and move once again in this place.

He told her she needed Crow, and Crow needed her.

Sani rested now. Hannah knew giving her the medicine wouldn't help if they had to flee unexpectedly, but the old woman was clearly in pain. There was no reason to make her suffer.

Movement caught Hannah's eye.

Hok'ee's eyes glowed in the dark.

Hannah's body relaxed. She moved past the ground-tied horses and mule to where Jack sat on a large rock. He insisted they move from the center of the canyon to a more protected side-area; this way, he could keep a lone watch.

She sat beside him. He shifted his rifle to cradle in his left arm.

"Hok'ee is here," she said. "He'll watch, too."

"I think you may be right about that."

"This place is restless." The chilled air caused her to shiver.

He put an arm around her, and she accepted his touch, leaning into him. "Why do you think that is?" he asked.

"Before the Long Walk, the army hunted the Navajo within these walls. They chopped hundreds of peach trees down, killed livestock, and destroyed homes. The people were left to starve or freeze to death. Surrender became the only option. The pain in the Diné is still raw. It was an incredible blessing that they were allowed to return, but the wounds are deep. Hastin is one who was changed by it. Now, with army rations likely to end soon, many are at odds with one another. My pa wanted to preserve what the Diné are, but in the end, some became as evil as the Anglo men who began this struggle."

"You sound like you're forgiving Hastin for being what he is."

"I saw my pa," she said quietly, glancing up at Jack. "When I was dead. It's not the end. He isn't suffering. The only one who suffers is me, because I miss him so much." Her voice caught and tears welled.

Jack shifted the rifle crosswise on his lap and brought a hand to her cheek, brushing at the wetness with his thumb. His lips came to hers, gentle, demanding nothing. His restraint and tenderness surprised her, for he seemed a man unaccustomed to it.

He leaned his forehead to hers, running a hand to her neck, the touch full of promise.

"You're bruised," he said softly.

She didn't want to admit just how sore her throat felt, but any type of movement set off waves of pain.

"I'm sorry once again that I left you and Sani," he continued. "I meant to ride ahead and deal with the situation before either of you got near it."

"Then how did you know to return?" She let Jack fold his arms around her, bringing her close, keeping her safe within his embrace.

"My grandparents came from Scotland; my *seanmhair*—my granny—from the Highlands. She had ... gifts, some of which she tried to teach me when I was young. She was known as a *taibhsear*. She had visions, sometimes of spirits, and she could see fetches, or doubles."

"You strike me as a man who doesn't concern himself with such things."

"It's not something I share with most." He tucked her closer. "As I rode away from you today, the wind picked up, and I looked to the sky. A pattern emerged in the clouds."

When he stopped, she nudged him. "Tell me."

With a low laugh, he shook his head. "I saw you, there in the clouds. I saw your face. And then, a bad feeling came over me, so strong I turned around immediately."

"You practice the sight through clouds?" Hannah smiled. "I've not heard that one."

"If you tell anyone, I'll deny it."

"Your secret is safe with me. You saved my life, Jack." She leaned back slightly to look up at him. "Thank you."

His gaze met hers. "I think you've bewitched me."

"It would be fitting if I did possess such powers, since it is Hallowtide."

"This was Granny's favorite time. She would light candles and leave spice cakes for the spirits, for all three days."

"You don't look Scottish, Jack."

"I'm Comanche and Mexican on my mama's side."

"You must have interesting customs at home."

"I suppose you want to come and study us. My mama was the product of a Comanche warrior and a Mexican slave. She was called Topsanna while she lived in the tribe, but when she married my pa, she adopted the name of Mary. He met her at a trading post in North Texas and bargained quite aggressively for her. My folks live in Springfield, Missouri. They raised me and my younger brothers, Callum and Kit, under fairly normal circumstances, away from the taint of our heathen blood."

Hannah sat upright. "You're not a heathen, Jack."

He smiled. "I know. My brothers and I all spent time with the Comanche. Mama conformed to white society but kept her heritage alive in private. Maybe I'll take you to meet her one day. I think she'd like you."

Unnerved by how easy it was to imagine a life with Jack, she countered nervously, "You're just being nice to me because I died today."

He brought a hand to her face and leaned forward to kiss her cheek. She closed her eyes and reveled in his touch. During her death, it was the physical sensations she missed the most. The warmth of Jack, the musky smell, the prickly stubble of his cheeks, all reminded her, achingly, how much she cherished it. What if she hadn't come back?

Turning her face, she brought her mouth to his, ignoring the twinges of discomfort from her throat. He was so careful with her that it emboldened her to press forward, instinct guiding her. Her persistence ignited—at long last—a fire in Jack, and Hannah held on tight as he kissed her with deep intentions and a passion that made her shiver clear down to her toes.

She clung to him, and Jack set the rifle beside them, then pushed her onto her back, the rocky platform barely giving them enough room. In the darkness, any shyness she might have felt disappeared. She learned his mouth with her mouth, she let her fingers thread into his hair, she encouraged the weight of him to lie fully atop her.

His hand slipped into the folds of her coat, and he began to touch her breast, causing her to gasp.

"Hannah, we shouldn't." But his head dipped low, and his mouth sought that same breast, still covered in clothing, but sensitive, nonetheless.

She writhed beneath him, then pulled his face to hers. "Can it be quick?"

"That's not how I want it to be with you."

"After today," she said, her voice barely a rasp, "we both know nothing is guaranteed." She kissed him soundly. "I want you, Crow."

She could feel his readiness pressed against her.

He groaned softly, and with one hand, unbuttoned the top of her shirt, pushed the camisole up, then put his mouth fully on her bared nipple. Her back arched as a jolt of pleasure shot through her. As he held her hips, his mouth came back to hers and took every last breath from her as she fumbled with his long coat to get his pants from him. In a frenzy, he helped her, then lifted her skirt and pulled her drawers clear down to her ankles. He covered her body with his, and entered her in one swift motion, pausing as she adjusted to him.

The pain was brief, quickly replaced with a mounting anticipation. He began to move, and she met him, thrust for thrust, holding tight as she climaxed. Jack's body moved in rhythm with her, filling her with everything he had to offer.

As they both tried to catch their breaths, the sensation of him against her made her feel deeply satisfied. He kissed her, raw and sensual, making her wish they were in a bed and could lie naked beside one another all night long.

He shifted from her. "I'm sorry, Hannah. I hope I didn't hurt you. Damn, I hope you're real, and not some fantastical dream I'm having."

She kissed his chin, then his cheek, then fully on the mouth. "It's every girl's dream, to be taken on a rock by a handsome stranger."

"I mean to change the *stranger* part, if you'll let me."

She whispered against his lips. "Only if you promise to do that to me again."

CHAPTER SIX

J ack spent the rest of the night with Hannah molded against him, snuggled in his arms, his legs on either side of her while he sat with his back against the cliffside and his rifle handy. Thankfully, she slept, but he didn't. He wouldn't let his guard down again. All night he kept watch, equally at peace, aroused, and vigilant for danger.

Loving Hannah in an explosive episode of passion had been unplanned, knocking the wind clean out of him. He'd wanted her—it had been there the moment he'd looked into her bright green eyes—but the last thing he wanted was to breach her boundaries after she'd been through so much with the loss of her pa, then her own death.

But when she responded to him with so much need, it had obliterated his self-control with one swift kick. Usually, he was more careful —he didn't spread his seed in carelessness. He had no need for bastard children. Fancy ladies knew how to take care of such things. And with others, he'd taken more care to prevent any … complications.

But not with Hannah.

And if that hadn't been enough to show him a force greater than both of them were at play, there'd been the damn tears. Stunned by the brief, intense encounter, emotions had welled up inside that left him on the verge of weeping. He'd quickly clamped down on it, making certain Hannah didn't see, for fear it might frighten her.

What woman wanted a man crying after loving her?

What the hell had happened to him?

I found Hannah.

Despite his mind telling him such things were hogwash, he knew that he'd been waiting for her his entire life.

HANNAH AWOKE WITH A START. STILL WITHIN JACK'S EMBRACE, THE chilled morning air made her nose cold. He dozed, but as she moved, he came awake.

"Mornin'," he said, and rubbed his face.

"Good morning." Stiff and sore, she shifted to sit upright.

He pulled her back and kissed her. "I like seeing you first thing."

She smiled, then grimaced. "What's that smell?" The odor carried the stench of death.

She moved from him and rounded the rocky outcrop to where the animals and Sani had been. Relief filled her when she spied the horses and mule, but panic replaced it when she saw no sign of the Navajo woman.

"Where is she?" she asked, making a sweep of the area. Jack did the same, the rifle in hand.

"Tracks lead that way," Jack said, indicating a path to the opposite cliff wall.

"Is she alone?"

"It seems so."

A thin sheen of smoke settled into the canyon floor.

"What is that smell, Jack?"

"You stay here," he said. "Let me go."

"No. Sani's in trouble." She moved past him, but he stopped her. She looked into his dark eyes, fathomless, like the black sheen of crow feathers. "Don't leave me alone, Jack."

Wordlessly, he agreed and quickly secured their camp. He tended the animals, ground-tying them in an area that would offer shade as the sun crept across the sky.

Hannah walked behind Jack, with no weapon in hand since Sani had taken the shotgun. The odor of burning flesh, be it animal or human, was so strong now that Hannah held a kerchief to her mouth and nose. They came to the sheer, red wall rising to the heavens and found a narrow crack.

Jack entered, and Hannah followed.

AS HE NEARED THE OPENING OF THE FISSURE ON THE OTHER SIDE, IT WAS as Jack feared. A thin Indian moved about, a fire blazing at the center with what appeared to be a sheep carcass burning. He caught sight of Sani, bound and gagged, a bright stain of blood soaked into the garment from the shoulder injury Hannah had tended the previous night.

She lived, but he suspected not for long.

Then, he saw Lopez, dozing some distance from the fire. From his ripped clothing and several visible wounds, it was obvious he'd fought Hok'ee, and was most definitely worse off for it. But he wasn't a prisoner of Hastin Yazhe.

Why?

"What's going on?" Hannah whispered from behind.

With no substantial coverage, either rock or foliage, Jack thought it too dangerous to exit the crack. But what if Hastin, or Lopez, decided to leave the enclosure? While there might be another exit, they could run right into Jack and Hannah.

He turned to face Hannah. "Sani is alive, but captive. I see an Indian, who I assume is Hastin."

"We need to get her," Hannah whispered, an urgency in her voice.

"Do you think he'll kill her?"

"Yes."

"Why?"

Hannah hesitated. "Sani and Hastin disagreed many moons ago, during the time of the Long Walk. So many of the Navajo were filled with such a deep sorrow that it ultimately bred vengeance. When Hastin embraced the evil, Sani abandoned him. She refused to acknowledge him."

"Acknowledge how?" Jack asked.

"Hastin is her brother."

Jack stared hard at Hannah. "Then why in tarnation would he kill her?"

"Hastin doesn't forgive."

"That's why she left us, isn't it?" he asked. "To deal with Hastin on her own?"

"I'm not certain of that. Sani agreed to help me because no one else in the tribe wanted anything to do with him. Neither did she, for that matter, but she respected my pa and understood how important it was for me to put his soul to rest. This has been at great distress to her."

"I still can't believe that Hastin will kill her."

"Maybe he won't, but I don't want to chance it."

He saw the shadow too late. A Navajo man slipped behind Hannah and rendered her unconscious with one blow. Jack grasped Hannah's limp body and wedged himself to protect her, slamming the Indian's nose with the butt of his hand. As blood spurted, the man sagged but the one behind him aimed a revolver in Jack's face.

Jack didn't move. He wouldn't risk Hannah's life, but he feared that none of them would make it out of this canyon alive.

By his calculation, it was October 31st.

Hallowe'en.

Perhaps it was fitting to meet the Maker on this day, since it happened to be his birthday.

CHAPTER SEVEN

H annah came awake, her eyes taking in the scene before her, and panic sank into her bones.

A body burned at the center of a huge blaze.

Not Jack. Please not Jack.

She lay on her side, feet tied, and hands bound behind her, leaving a painful ache in her right shoulder. Hastin Yazhe moved past her, just as she remembered him—gaunt, his short black hair pushed back with a red cloth worn high on his forehead, and the same sinister scowl that had scared her from the first moment she and her pa had encountered him more than two years ago.

She glanced around, reluctant to move her head lest she alert Hastin that she was awake. The throbbing in her skull reminded her she'd been struck.

Was Jack already dead? Was it his body in the fire? She squeezed her eyes to block the wave of grief.

She heard Sani's voice, speaking Navajo. She and Hastin argued, and Sani attempted to bargain for their lives. The name Crow came up repeatedly.

Relief washed through Hannah. *Jack lived!* At least, for now.

But Sani pressed onward, all but threatening Hastin with the presence of Crow.

No, Sani. It will only cause Hastin to kill Jack faster.

Hannah moved, and succeeded in catching Hastin's attention, effectively ending Sani's conversation.

The Navajo man came to her and squatted near her face. "Hannah of Walter Dobbin, you have left me no choice."

His breath smelled of whiskey, his deerskin breeches stained with blood. A silver bracelet encircled his wrist, and Hannah knew he'd stolen it from Sani. Tension twisted in her gut. If he killed Sani and kept the jewelry, would her soul become caught between worlds as her father's was?

Hannah lifted her gaze to his, the fire casting a pale light into the deep darkness of the night enveloping them. "There is no peace for the wicked, Hastin Yazhe."

"That is where you are wrong." He leaned closer. "I am quite at peace."

"The spirits are out tonight. Even you can't protect your soul."

His face split into a grin filled with malice. "You and your father come to live with the Navajo, and you think you know us. You know no such thing. You are just like the white men who sent us away from our homeland. You are not welcome. And now, because you cannot heed my advice, I must kill you as I did your father."

"It is *you* who is no longer Navajo," she replied. "You do not practice the Blessing Way. You are corrupt. You're an abomination."

He laughed. "A white girl telling me how to be one of the People. I will save you for last. You will make an excellent powder."

He left her. *An excellent powder?* What did that mean? Dark whispers in her mind told her, but she didn't want to believe it. There was talk of corpse powder, always in hushed tones, the fear of it palpable among those who spoke of it. Were there actually Navajo who made such a substance?

With mounting anxiety, Hannah suspected that Hastin dared to practice even more sinister arts than she'd assumed all along.

THE CROW AND THE COYOTE

JACK COULD SEE HANNAH'S FEET ON THE OPPOSITE SIDE OF THE HUGE FIRE from where he sat, immobile. He was grateful when she moved, reassuring him she lived. He sat upright, but his hands were bound behind him and his feet roped together.

A body burned in the fire, replacing the charred remains of the sheep from earlier.

"That is Ramirez," Lopez said.

Jack's blood ran cold. His brothers chased Ramirez. They'd split up outside of Phoenix when the trails diverged. Jack took this route because he knew Lopez was the more ruthless of the two. He was right.

"I take it you and Ramirez didn't see eye-to-eye," Jack said.

"I don't take kindly to a double-cross."

"Why burn the body?"

Are Cal and Kit near? He wasn't a praying man, but he'd say a prayer if it kept his brothers safe.

"That is Yazhe's idea." Lopez still nursed wounds on his arms, face, and neck from Hok'ee.

"Why are you with Yazhe?" Jack asked.

"I guess you call it black magic."

Jack scanned the area around the blaze. He had sight of Hannah. He wished she were closer. Sani was also visible. The three Navajo men who'd jumped him sat together to his far left alongside Hastin.

"I have been trying to decide what to do with you, Crow," Lopez said, kneeling before him. "You have been on my trail for some time. I admire that. In fact, did you know that I left that gringo woman for you outside of Phoenix? It was my gift to you."

When Jack found the woman, beaten and bleeding, she'd barely been alive. Lopez had mutilated the husband and shot two children in the head. Jack had watched the life drain from the woman's eyes. He couldn't blame her for not wanting to stay, after the unspeakable loss of her family, but still, he'd hoped to save her, to salvage something from the violence that Lopez practiced so casually.

There were times he wished his memory would fade, to erase the atrocities that weighed heavy on his soul, but those moments of self-ishness left him quickly. Without him, and men like him, there would be no one to stop the likes of Lopez.

Whatever might come of this night, he wouldn't let the Mexican walk out of here alive.

CHAPTER EIGHT

H annah struggled to a sitting position and caught sight of Jack across the fire. She nodded to him, and his hooded gaze softened slightly.

She coughed and tried again not to inhale. The acrid stink from the burning body filled the air, nauseating her. It smelled like an animal cooked too long, with a sharp metallic stench rolling off it.

Her eyes watered, and the tears threatened to become real.

She could see the three Navajo who had jumped her and Jack earlier—Ahiga, Manaba and Tse. She didn't know them well, but they were also dissenters. The first two were middle-aged, having suffered through the Long Walk, while Tse was Manaba's son.

Would they kill Jack and Sani before placing them in the fire? Or would they be burned alive?

Hannah thought losing her pa had done her in, but now she desired to live. Even more, she desired Jack to live.

Watching him, she wished they'd had more time.

She hung her head and suppressed a sob.

Her eyes snapped up when she heard a gasp from the Navajo men. In fast succession, they all dropped to the ground, arrows protruding from their chests.

Hastin dove toward her. She fell to the side and tried to scoot away from him.

He yanked her to her feet, his arm around her throat choking her as he kept spinning them around, clearly not certain from what direction the attack came.

"I will kill her!" he yelled.

She felt the point of a knife in her side. Her legs threatened to collapse as she sucked in desperately needed air. Hastin would end her life if she couldn't get away.

Could Jack bring me back from the dead a second time?

From the inky night came two men with dark features and a lethal glow in their eyes. They both held pistols, one in each hand.

Jack?

Were they ghosts?

Or crows in the night ...

Hastin held her tighter. With her hands twisted behind her, she had no weapon, no way to fight him.

She sunk her teeth into the flesh on his arm, drawing blood. A bellow came from him, and she slid to the ground.

Gunfire erupted over her, and she wished she could cover her ears as the crows killed Hastin Yazhe.

Booted feet moved past.

"Find Jack," one of the crows said.

Hannah grunted as she rolled so she could see where they went.

Searching across the fire, Jack was gone. All that greeted her was the heat from the fire, the foulness of an over-cooked corpse, and Hastin's lifeless body several feet away.

She noticed Sani beyond, still bound and gagged, appearing frantic and upset.

"Sani," she yelled. "Are you all right?"

The Navajo woman nodded.

All they could do was wait until Jack or the crows returned and freed them, or the man Jack hunted found them. Terrified, she knew this time Lopez would kill her for good.

She thought she heard something, far beyond in the dark. The fire began to die down, the charred skin sunken onto the bones of the body that had been cooked for much of the day. Blood oozed from Hastin's unmoving body, but Hannah couldn't muster any remorse for the man.

Shadows moved just beyond, and Hannah held her breath, fearing that it wouldn't be Jack. Winged creatures flew. Logic told her it was bats. She blinked several times, certain her mind played tricks.

No.

She had no doubt she witnessed crows.

Jack and two men emerged from the haze hanging in the gloom, the fluttering of feathers dispersing in their wake.

"Jack," she whispered.

He came to her. Brandishing a knife, he made swift work of releasing her. Time slowed, as if in a dream, and she turned to him. In his eyes she saw gratitude and felt transported to a place of deep green and moist Mother Earth. She'd never been to Scotland, but in this moment, Jack seemed to embody his homeland.

"I'm glad you're alive," he said. He laid his roughened hand gently against her cheek and kissed her with such tenderness that tears rolled down her face.

He stood and carefully helped her to her feet.

"I want you to meet my brothers," he said, wrapping an arm around her waist in support.

She looked to the men who had killed Hastin and released Sani from her ropes. The resemblance to Jack was uncanny.

"You're all crows," she murmured.

Jack made a sound of amusement. "That's Callum, and the young one is Kit."

Neither wore hats, and their dark hair rivaled Jack's.

"Miss." Callum nodded in her direction.

"This is Hannah Dobbin," Jack said, "and that's Sani."

Kit grinned. "Pleased to make your acquaintance, Miss Dobbin. Jack seems to have picked up a pretty pebble along the way."

Hannah smiled, then moved to Sani. "How is your wound?"

"I will live." Sani squared her shoulders. "Something must be done about Hastin."

Hannah nodded, then looked to Jack. "Lopez?" she asked.

"Dead." His jaw flexed and his gaze hardened. Gone were the otherworldly fields of Scottish green; in its place was the harsh reality of the deeds he—and his brothers—were required to commit. In that moment, she saw clearly the Comanche that pulsed in him.

"How?" she asked.

Jack's gaze softened and she couldn't look away, so breathtaking was the transformation. Hardened by the life he led, both in body and spirit, she sensed he rarely let his guard down. But when he did, he was beautiful.

"Hok'ee brought me a knife," he said. "I was able to free myself. When the arrows took out the three, I knew it was Kit. Lopez ran, but I was able to follow."

"He could've killed you," Hannah said.

"Then, I would've counted on you to bring me back."

A stark intimacy wrapped tightly around them, and embarrassment swept over her that the others should witness this exchange between them.

"I'm thinking there's more to this story," Callum said, "but for now we best leave this place. It is Hallowe'en. The spirits will be about. What do you hear, Kit?"

"I hear *him*," Kit said, turning around.

Hok'ee watched from the murky shadows, his yellow eyes glowing.

"The cross," Hannah said, but Jack stopped her as she prepared to bolt to Hastin's body and search his belongings.

"No need," Callum said. "I know where it is."

Hannah watched as Jack's brother sorted through a pile of leather pouches, located the item, then returned and placed it in her hand.

"How did you do that?" she asked him.

"Jack'll tell you. I think you're gonna be around for a while."

A deep knowing in her heart told her much the same but she didn't say it aloud.

38

The heavy, silver cross filled her palm. At last, she had her pa's memento, so very dear to him.

"What now?" Jack asked quietly.

Her eyes met his, and realization hit that she didn't know how to release a spirit.

She shifted her gaze to Hok'ee. He approached and everyone backed away, then Hannah knelt to greet the animal.

He sniffed the metal, then sat before her. The last embers of the fire shone in his eyes.

"I love you, Pa. It's time for you to go. It's time to be free."

A memory came to her of a time when she was young, before her mama had died of fever, when the three of them had shared the joy of a family.

She smiled despite the tears welling in her eyes. "She's here," she whispered, feeling the essence of her mother wrap around her. "Mama will help."

The cross had been a gift, from her mama to her pa, on the day they married. Her pa had spoken of it many times in the years that followed. He'd always cherished it, but after she had passed, he'd been almost obsessed with it.

Hok'ee licked her cheeks and she hugged him; then, with an affectionate nudge, he stepped back. With one last look, he turned and disappeared into the night.

Goodbye, Pa.

CHAPTER NINE

J ack, Cal and Kit spent several hours taking care of the macabre encampment of Hastin Yazhe. But first, they settled Hannah and Sani back in the main canyon, away from the dead bodies and angry spirits in residence. Jack knew this because Kit's uncanny gift of *hearing* alerted them. They worked swiftly, burying Hastin and the three Navajo killed by Kit's arrows. When it came to Lopez, done in by Jack and the knife Hok'ee had brought him, it was agreed they would wrap the body and take it with them. The bounty still needed to be collected, and they were uncertain whether they'd be able to recoup on Ramirez.

"I've never seen a man burnt to a crisp," Cal said.

"A strange end for Ramirez," Kit said. "We lost his trail not long after we split up, but Callum sniffed him out."

Cal's ability to scout future events in his dreams had come in handy more than once. Jack and his brothers kept their *skills* to themselves, but whatever it was they'd inherited from their Scottish grandmother had kept them alive in many a dangerous situation.

Cal recovered a pouch of black, grainy powder from Hastin's belongings. "What the hell is this?" he asked, holding a sample in his hand.

"It was Hastin's specialty," Jack replied. "Corpse powder."

Cal grimaced and deposited the particles back into the leather sack. "Why would he need this?" He slapped his hand against his leg several times to rid himself of the residue.

"It's too bad Granny's gone," Kit said. "She might've known."

"Regardless of what it was for," Jack said, "I think we need to take care how we dispose of it."

"What do you recommend?" Cal asked.

"I've sage with me. We bury it at least three feet then burn the sage atop it."

Once the task was accomplished, a pungent and woodsy aroma surrounded them, cleansing the land and pushing away the whispers of the dead. Kit said as much.

"I think Cal and I can handle Lopez's body," Kit said to Jack. "We'll return it to Fort Defiance. I imagine you should help Hannah Dobbin and the Old One return to the Navajo."

Jack nodded. "I might take some time ..."

"A holiday?" Cal laughed. "Did you hear that, Kit? Jack's gonna chase a skirt full-time."

"Is she worth it?" Kit asked.

"Yep." And Jack knew it was true, clear to his bones.

HANNAH AWOKE AS JACK'S BODY PRESSED AGAINST HERS, WARMING HER backside. His hand rested on her hip, and he kissed her cheek. She shifted to face him, then lifted the sheepskin blanket to include him.

"Thank you, Jack, for all your help," she whispered.

His mouth came to hers, at first soft, then with more heat. He brought his arms around her and held her close, his lips pressed to her forehead. As she settled against him, she felt his restraint, likely due to their lack of privacy; but her body hummed with the need to be alone with him. Her mind wandered to what it would be like to lie skin to skin, to learn him in ways she'd never desired to do with another.

"There'll be time for that," he said quietly.

"Promise?"

His mouth found hers again, igniting a deep longing in her.

"I promise."

CHAPTER TEN

Six months later

Jack guided his horse into Cañon de Chelly, Hannah trailing behind upon her own animal. He'd promised her a visit to Sani, who now resided within, before the babe arrived.

About four months along, Hannah's belly was just starting to bulge, and now that she was past the sickness period, he agreed to the journey. They'd been living in a rented room in Tuba City, within the boundaries of the Navajo—and the Hopi—while Hannah finished writing and collating the work she and her father had started. But after this trip, Jack insisted they move to Prescott, some 300 miles to the southwest. He wanted Hannah to have a decent doctor to deliver the babe. His child.

The Crow would soon be a father.

The thought made him immensely happy.

His folks would visit later in the year, and Cal and Kit appeared from time to time. Jack hadn't waited to marry Hannah. When he'd heard the circuit judge was on his way to Prescott two months ago, he arranged to have the man intercepted and brought to his betrothed.

He'd been damn determined to wed her. Hannah Dobbin was wrapped tight into his soul, and he knew he'd spend his life offering her everything he had to give, opening his heart in ways he never had. And there was no way he'd let his child be born without a proper father.

On this beautiful spring day, they found Sani's homestead tucked beside a burgeoning orchard of peach trees.

He dismounted and helped Hannah from her horse. She smiled and he drank in her sage-green eyes.

On impulse, he removed his hat and kissed her. "I love you, Hannah."

"Did you see it written in the clouds?" she teased.

As he often did, he rested a hand upon her belly. "It'll be a girl."

Delight lit her eyes. "Are you certain?"

"No, but Callum dreamt it."

"And she may just be born on your birth day, if she times it right."

"Another Hallowe'en birth," he said. "She'd make the Boggs' family name proud."

Grinning, she returned his kiss, then turned to find Sani, who now lived with a sister and a nephew in two nearby hogans.

Staying back, he watched his wife walk away from him. She removed her hat as her long skirt collected red dust along the edges. She was a vision to him, having come to him in this place. His luck had never been better than when he'd tracked Lopez here and found Hannah instead.

On the breeze, her words floated back to him.

"I love you, Crow."

THE CROW AND THE BEAR

When no one will help Jennie Livingstone enter a haunted ravine to find her papa, she must accept the aid of enigmatic bounty hunter Callum Boggs, sometimes called The Crow.

CHAPTER ONE

Silverton, Colorado
October 1878

"Y ou're not listening to me." Jennie Livingstone scanned the gentlemen gathered in the common room at the Silverton Hotel. "This absence isn't normal for Papa."

"We know you're worried, Jennie," an older man named Sharply said. "But Ben knows these hills. He's not missing. He's just late."

"No." She shook her head. "Something's wrong."

She looked in turn at each one of them—strong men who had spent their lives mining and prospecting. She trusted them, knowing they were her papa's friends. "Won't any of you help me search for him?" In desperation, she added, "I'll pay you."

Silence engulfed the room.

"I'll help you, miss."

Jennie spun around at the deep timber of a man's voice. With her back to the entryway, she hadn't noticed his arrival.

Dark eyes greeted her from beneath a well-worn Stetson. Tall, he filled the space he occupied, drowning out the presence of every other man in the room. His nose was reddened from the biting wind that had descended into the valley during the night, but while he had the look of an Indian, Jennie was put in mind of the crows that congregated around the home she shared with her father on the edge of town.

"Who're you?" one of the miners asked.

"Name's Callum Boggs. I'm a bounty hunter from Missouri. There's talk Ben Livingstone went to Silas Ravine."

Jennie gasped as agitation overtook the room. "How do you know that?" she asked.

"I have my sources." Mister Boggs removed his hat. "Is that why none of these gentlemen will help you?" His eyes swept the room.

Stunned, Jennie turned back to Sharply, his grizzled features matched by the dirt-stained clothing he wore. "Did Ben go to Silas Ravine?"

The old man exhaled deeply. "He might've said that's where he was headed."

"Is that why he didn't take me with him?"

"I expect so."

Anger filled her. And fear. Her papa knew the stories about the ravine, knew the tragedy that could befall anyone who dared to go there. She always traveled with him into the hills when he scouted ore veins, but this time, he'd insisted that she stay back because she'd not been feeling well.

I shouldn't have let him go.

Tears threatened, but she shored up her courage. Crying over spilled milk wasn't going to find Papa. As she searched the room full of men, all avoided her gaze.

Except one.

Bounty hunter Callum Boggs.

"Aren't you afraid of Silas Ravine, as all these men are?" Her hand swept the room.

Narrowing his eyes, the barest hint of a smile played across his mouth. "No, miss, I'm not."

"Then, you're hired."

He acknowledged his new employment status with a slight nod while planting the Stetson atop his head. "We best get started."

Jennie wondered how this man had come from nowhere to help her, but she kept her curiosity in check. Perhaps heading into the hills with a stranger was lunacy, but Silas Ravine—the site of numerous missing men and reputed to be haunted—left her with few options. She could go alone. She certainly knew these mountains, the hills and valleys and streams, but a frisson of unease shivered down her spine. She was as afraid of Silas Ravine as any of the men here. If she must go—and for her papa she would—then making a bargain with a warrior of Hades was the best course of action.

Possibly the *only* course of action.

CHAPTER TWO

C al walked with Jennie Livingstone to her home at the end of Reese Street, flipping his jacket collar up to ward off the late-October chill despite the clear day. With the immense Rocky Mountains surrounding the town of Silverton on all sides, direct sunlight wouldn't last for long. Jagged peaks covered with snow hinted that winter never truly left this place.

He shouldered his knapsack and drew a sidelong glance at the intrepid young woman.

It was her. The one he'd dreamt about.

She was even more striking in person. Brown hair pulled loosely from her face in a haphazard bun, a smattering of freckles on her nose, deep green eyes the color of a Scottish forest. Gazing at her, it had been difficult to remain focused on the task at hand.

He'd come in search of an outlaw named Harley Jessup, but he couldn't deny he was curious about *her*, the woman in his visions, she who was to guide him into the mountains. His Scottish grandmother had taught him the ways of dream forecasting and it often guided him on manhunts.

He hadn't known her first name. "Jennie."

"Yes?"

He hadn't meant to say it aloud. To cover his slip, he asked, "How long have you and your father lived in Silverton?"

"About three years."

"Is your mother here? Any siblings?"

"I'm an only child. My mother died when I was three. I don't really remember her." She watched him. "Why have you come all the way from Missouri?"

"My ma and pa live in Springfield, but I was recently in Arizona Territory."

"How long have you been a bounty hunter?"

He skirted around a mud hole. "About five years now."

"Are you good at it?"

He couldn't suppress an amused smile. "Good enough."

"I suppose that will be assurance enough."

"Worried you won't get what you pay for?"

She laughed, the air turning white from her breath. "I plan to keep an eye on my investment. Have you ever been in the Rocky Mountains before?"

"No."

A buckboard ambled past, the man nodding at Jennie. "I'm only taking you along to fight off the bears, and other things."

He frowned. "What kind of 'other things'?"

"Not everything can be seen with your eyes or heard with your ears."

"Sounds like a puzzle."

"Are you easily spooked?"

He grinned. "No."

"That's good," she replied, clearly agitated. "And I just want to state for the record that if you try anything, I'll kill you."

Cal stopped walking, stunned by her casual statement. It was clear she wasn't easily pushed around. Despite being a petite woman, she carried herself with a sturdy constitution, one he couldn't deny appealed to him immensely.

"I can assure you that I'm not here to take advantage of a woman," he said.

She watched him with a stern expression, then nodded. "Fine. I'll choose to trust you, then. I need a man I can rely on."

"You can count on me, Jennie."

Her expression softened and she turned away, continuing down the street.

Despite the rocky start, Cal decided he liked her.

CHAPTER THREE

J ennie guided her bay roan gelding onto the path leading from
Silverton, his grayish coat matching the overcast morning. Her
new companion—Mister Boggs—rode beside her on a stock horse
he purchased in town, the animal's powerful hindquarters flexing
with each step. They both had bedrolls, extra blankets, and saddlebags
stuffed with supplies. Her trusty mule, Maisie, trailed behind, loaded
with two small canvas tents, food, ammunition, and medical supplies.

She had a Winchester in a boot and a Colt tucked into her bags. She
noticed Mister Boggs kept a Colt as well, side-holstered for easy
release. He also had a long rifle—a Henry from the look of it.
Although an older weapon, she knew from her papa it offered strong
repeating action at close range. A bounty hunter would likely have
need of such a firearm, but she suspected this type of protection
would prove useless in Silas Ravine.

Boggs brought his horse level with hers. A cold wind greeted them
as they left Silverton and headed north toward the mining camp of
Eureka. Jennie tugged her hat down, her hair in a braid down her
back. She was dressed practically—wool trousers, boots, flannel shirt,
long underwear, thick socks, a heavy duster, and a red scarf she'd
woven herself.

"Where're you from?" he asked.

"I was born in Philadelphia. After Mama died, an aunt raised me. Papa came and went. When I was about ten years old, he came west to work as a surveyor in the Denver area. He's educated as a geologist. I begged to come with him, and he let me. We went from place to place—Virginia City, California, Arizona Territory—but I think Silverton is his favorite."

"It sounds as if you're well-traveled, Jennie Livingstone."

"It suits me to have a change of scenery." She glanced at his hard profile. Was she loco for setting off into the wilderness with a man she didn't know? While she had hoped to have one of the local miners accompany her, it was abundantly clear that Boggs was more suited to this expedition than a man such as Sharply, especially now that the destination was Silas Ravine.

"I hope you don't mind me asking," she continued, "but are you Indian?"

"Would it bother you if I was?"

"No."

"My ma is Comanche. My pa is Scottish."

Watching Boggs as they collected supplies and gear yesterday, his actions precise yet restrained, spoke of an inherent strength missing from the men in town. While they were a tough lot, they lacked grace. Jennie wondered if all Comanche were like Callum Boggs.

"Have you ever been to Scotland?" she asked.

He nodded. "When I was a boy. My pa is from the Inverness area. He took all of us."

"Who's 'all of us'?"

"My ma and my two brothers."

"Are they bounty hunters, too?"

"For a time, yep. My older brother, Jack, was married earlier this year and is about to become a father, so I'm guessing his days of manhunts are over. I don't think Hannah would like it, and truth be told, he never wants to leave her."

"He must love her very much."

"I'd say so."

She guided her horse past a boulder in the path. "And what of your other brother?"

"Kester's the runt. He's roaming Arizona Territory at the moment."

"Does he look like you?"

Boggs frowned at her. "It's been said my brothers and I have such a resemblance that people can't tell us apart."

"Then Kester's no runt," she murmured.

"I do believe you just complimented me, Miss Livingstone."

"I'm sure I'm not the first woman to say something ... nice ... about you."

"You'd be surprised."

When she looked at him, raising her eyebrows in question, a look of derision crossed his features but was soon gone. "Half-breeds don't always garner warm welcomes," he added softly.

"Not everyone is ignorant."

He held her gaze longer than courtesy dictated, causing her to look away, momentarily flustered. Why in the world would she care about the prejudices against this man?

Breaking the awkward tension, he said, "Can you tell me why Silas Ravine is so feared?"

Jennie considered the question. If she told him the rumors, would he refuse to go any farther with her? She'd traveled these hills enough that she could certainly continue alone. Couldn't she? Her chest squeezed as her heartbeat raced. In that moment, she knew she desperately needed this man to stay close.

"Right about the time my papa and I came to town, a criminal named Harley Jessup had been caught and placed in the jail. While awaiting a trial, he managed to escape. Some say a local fancy woman helped him. He disappeared into the mountains, and his trail went cold."

"So he escaped?"

"Unfortunately, he did. But then word came that he was in Silas Ravine. The Atkins brothers live up that way, and they reported seeing him. It was said that Jessup froze to death in a freakish storm that descended on Hallowtide."

"I see." Boggs appeared to brood, which Jennie didn't understand.

She plowed ahead anyway. "I don't know if you've ever spent time in a mining community, but there can be a great deal of superstition. The following spring, men began to trickle into the ravine because rumor had it there was a large vein beyond anyone's wildest dreams. That bred a lot of secrecy about the area. After a time, all the men who'd gone to stake a claim had never returned. So a posse was sent to investigate."

"What happened?"

"Only one man returned, and the story he told frightened everyone."

Boggs settled back into his saddle, the leather creaking in response. "Try me."

"They'd searched for evidence of the bodies but could find none. When nightfall came, they were forced to make camp. During the night they heard voices but couldn't see anyone. An older man in the group began choking, then died suddenly."

"That hardly merits a supernatural slant."

Jennie took in the panorama of ponderosa pine and juniper trees, a veritable Garden of Eden. "I agree. But the man who survived—his name was Wyatt, I think—claimed that a mist descended, and shadows began to flit past them. Some of the men drew guns. When the attack came, Wyatt was knocked out."

"Convenient."

"What are you saying?"

"Did it ever occur to anyone that Wyatt killed the men in the posse himself?"

The realization dawned on Jennie. "Why would he do that?"

"Can't say, but maybe he wanted access to the claim."

"But he's since left Silverton. From what my papa said, he was quite delirious after, bordering on madness."

Boggs watched her. "Why?"

"Papa never told me all the details, but I've heard from others in town. The men's bodies were mutilated, their eyes gouged out ... and ... and on a nearby rock were piled organs ripped from the bodies."

Jennie took a fortifying breath. She didn't like talking about this, especially now that her father had supposedly entered that place.

"Has anyone been to the ravine since then?"

Jennie brought her gaze to Boggs and saw compassion reflected, despite his gunmetal eyes. "Yes. Of course. There've been men from time to time who ventured there. None of them ever returned." *And now her papa hadn't, either.*

"So, there's no one who's seen the comings and goings into this ravine?"

Jennie inhaled the crisp autumn air, seeking to wash the fear from her body. "The Atkins brothers still live in the valley up ahead. They don't enter the ravine, either. They're just as scared as anyone else."

"Are they dangerous?"

"No, I don't believe so. Augustus lives alone and is a bit off. His brother, Lemuel, lives farther up with his wife, Betsy. They keep to themselves and don't come to town much, but they've spoken of strange happenings in the valley near the entrance to Silas Ravine— mutilated animals, strange markings on the rocks, trees that have been stripped of bark in unnatural ways."

"Everyone stays away based on these tales?"

Jennie nodded.

"Why did your father go there?"

Jennie glanced behind her to check on Maisie. "The vein, of course. It's said that Silas Ravine has one of the biggest lodes in the San Juan Mountains. I suppose his curiosity finally got the better of him. Prospecting can be like a siren's call."

"Like a woman you can't put out of your mind."

Jennie wondered if such a woman existed for Callum Boggs, but she kept her thought to herself. She scanned the magnificent scenery— high mountains blanketed with dense woodlands and patches of oak brush; a clear waterfall flowing across a granite escarpment.

"Your pa may just be holed up somewhere, investigating a

promising vein, caught up in the excitement and not realizing he's past due."

She knew that was the logical explanation, and she sincerely hoped it would turn out to be true. Boggs appeared skeptical as to the dark curse that somehow hung over Silas Ravine, but Jennie knew that there was something more to the place.

Simon had told her.

But she couldn't tell Boggs about Simon. He'd label her daft and possibly refuse to continue helping her.

The townsfolk had spoken in whispers of her from time to time, but never to her face. Ben Livingstone was well-liked and respected, and those sentiments naturally extended to his daughter. She had worked hard to help her papa, apprenticing at his side, learning about the shape of valleys, the coloration of rock, the slant of ridges that might indicate veins of everything from copper to silver to gold.

But she also had help. She'd spoken of it once to Ben, but when he laughed at her, she never uttered another word. She'd never quite figured out how the townsfolk spread gossip of her but suspected it was the time she 'spoke' in a forest with her allies. Someone must have overheard.

"You could be right," she finally replied.

"But you'll ride into the hills anyway?"

"These valleys are familiar to me. Having second thoughts, Boggs?"

"About you? No."

Jennie watched him a smidge longer than she should've, her heartbeat accelerating. She'd been courted by several men since her arrival in Silverton at the age of sixteen, but she'd been hard-pressed to be swayed by their affections and amorous overtures. Her papa had even kept her under lock and key at times, deterring the more aggressive ones. She wasn't ignorant of men and what they wanted—Silverton boasted numerous saloons and she was acquainted with several of the local ladies, whether her papa approved or not.

But Boggs's quiet countenance and controlled masculinity made her consider what women throughout time had confronted—throwing all caution to the wind for the sake of passion.

She pursed her lips together and turned away from him, chastising herself for entertaining such silly, girlish thoughts. She shifted her focus to Papa. If he were in trouble, he wouldn't have much time. Not if an early winter storm struck. It was late October. It could happen. He shouldn't have gone out this late in the season.

She hoped she could find him.

And she hoped that when she did, it wouldn't be in Silas Ravine.

CHAPTER FOUR

C al knew about the cabin before they saw it, not because of his talent of sight—which only came to him during dreams anyway; it was Jack who could divine while awake—but because tendrils of smoke could be seen far in advance, a sure sign of a fire in use. Jennie had skirted the mining settlement of Eureka, instead heading straight into a valley and the obscurity of the mountains.

Cal rode ahead and cut her off. "Stay behind me."

"Why?"

"Settlement ahead."

"I know. It's probably Augustus."

"Stay behind me," he repeated. He pulled the Henry from the scabbard and rested it across his thighs as he let the animal pick its way along the pathway.

A wooden building came into view, well-kept with a narrow porch and one window. Smoke spiraled upward from the stone fireplace.

Cal halted his horse. "Hello the house," he yelled.

The door cracked open. "Who're you?"

"Augustus, it's Jennie Livingstone."

Thankfully, she didn't try to sidle past Cal. He'd have cut her off anyhow, no matter that she knew the occupant.

The door opened farther and a man with a dark, unkempt beard peeked out. He held a shotgun, which Cal noticed he didn't immediately set aside.

"Who's that you're with, Jennie?" asked Augustus.

"This is Callum Boggs. He's helping me search for my father. Have you seen him?"

"Nah. Not since summer."

"Are you certain? He planned to come this way. He probably would've been through here ten days ago."

"Sorry, Jennie. I ain't seen him."

Cal sensed Jennie's frustration behind him.

"Are you well, Augustus?" she asked. "Do you need anything?"

Cal didn't like the fact that the man still hadn't put the gun down.

"I'm fine, Miss Jennie. You best be moving along with that fella of yours." He gripped the weapon in his hands and looked straight at Cal. "You best stay away from the ravine. Jennie'll tell you why."

"Let's go, Boggs," she said quietly from behind. Her horse began picking its way along a path parallel to the cabin.

Cal scanned the cabin's location, always keeping Augustus in his line of vision. He kept himself between Jennie and the curmudgeon's shotgun.

Once they were out of sight, they were forced into single file, the mule trailing Jennie's horse. When the passage finally opened up, Cal pushed his mount to a gallop and reined in beside her. The trail was still narrow and his leg brushed against hers, causing her gaze to flick to his. He enjoyed the flush on her cheeks.

"Do you think Augustus lied about Ben?" he asked.

"Maybe. If Papa was really headed for the ravine, I imagine he would've sneaked past the cabin."

Cal nodded, thinking the same.

They rode through the tundra until nightfall, although sunlight had been scarce for several hours. But Jennie wouldn't stop until forced to do so.

She was efficient in setting up camp, and soon enough, two canvas tents were erected side-by-side in a flat clearing. Cal made a fire while Jennie tended the horses and Maisie, picketing them in an area with grass still in abundance. Within this valley they were buffered from the wind and the chilled weather hadn't quite reached the vegetation yet.

Cal was weary, so heated beans in a pot hung from an iron tripod over the fire. Water would round out the meal. He wondered if Jennie would complain.

She trudged up to the fire, removed her hat and sat on the bare ground, folding her legs beneath her.

He spooned the food onto a tin plate and handed it to her. "It's not fancy, but it's hot."

"Smells wonderful." She lost no time in consuming the meal. She downed a cup of water then drank another. "When I'm with Ben it's usually salt pork and hard biscuits." She cleared her throat. "May I ask how you came to know that Ben is in Silas Ravine?"

Cal rarely confided his abilities to anyone. There was never any reason, but he decided to take a chance on Jennie. "I'm able to see events in my dreams before they happen."

"Truly?" She gave him her undivided attention, and it pleased him that she didn't laugh his statement off outright.

"My Scottish ancestry, I suppose. Before my granny died, she guided me."

"Did you dream about my father?"

He nodded.

"How could that be?" she asked. "Do you know him?"

"No."

"Then why would you randomly dream about him?"

The warm, sweet smell of burning juniper reminded him of nights with his brothers, filled with the freedom of living in the wilderness. "I've been hunting Harley Jessup in my dreams. He's in Silas Ravine, along with Ben Livingstone."

"But Jessup is dead. Does that mean my papa is too?"

"What I see isn't always entirely clear, but even you can admit that Jessup might not have frozen to death as was reported. As for your father, I honestly don't know."

Jennie paused, firelight caressing her smooth skin, then asked in a soft voice, "Did you dream about me?"

He poked a stick into the fire to avoid looking her in the eye, a sudden discomfort overtaking him. "Yes."

"Am I what you expected?" Her voice drifted across the space between them, heating his belly like a fine whiskey.

Unbidden, his mind wandered to the treasures hidden beneath the heavy layers of clothing she wore. "No."

"I'm not sure how I should take that."

Realizing his error, he added, "You're a lot prettier in person."

A smile tugged at the edges of her mouth. "I hope you're not a charlatan, Boggs."

"I don't lie, Jennie. And you can call me Cal."

CHAPTER FIVE

J ennie awoke before dawn and tended to personal matters in the woods while she had a modicum of privacy. During the night, she'd slept lightly and wondered how, through the thin walls of the canvas tent, Boggs didn't snore. Even now, as she moved about, she heard nothing from his tent.

Could he really *know* things from his dreams? The idea intrigued her.

She also felt a tug deep in her stomach every time he looked at her.

She set about stoking the fire. Once she had a flame going, she used the grinder to pummel the coffee beans, added them to the pot along with water and hung it from the tripod.

She jumped when the little sprite appeared. "I wish you wouldn't sneak up on me, Simon." Her hand splayed across her chest as she sought to quiet her nerves.

The short, squat man sat down next to her and tugged at his russet-colored cap. He wore a red thick wool coat and miner's boots. His stubby fingers scratched his face and he smirked. "Why are you traveling with that man?"

"You mean Cal?" she whispered, not wanting to disturb the man in question.

"He's called The Crow, and he brings a different energy here."

"Is that bad?" Worry flooded Jennie. Had she been wrong to let Boggs accompany her?

Simon lost a bit of his bluster, his shoulders sagging. "No. He's not a bad man."

Jennie couldn't stop the smile from reaching her mouth.

Simon grimaced at her. "Quit acting like a woman in love."

"I am not," she defended, a bit shocked by his pronouncement. While Callum Boggs was no doubt handsome—exuding an inherent strength that stirred excitement within her as if she hung from a precipice—she wasn't in need of a beau. She'd begun to think of late that marriage might not be in the cards for her since she enjoyed the freedom to come and go as she pleased. It also meant that she could care for her papa. If she had a husband, she would have to leave her father.

"Why don't you like him?" she asked her friend.

"The Crow walks the ancient pathways. He's a seer. He'll disrupt the flow."

"Isn't that a good thing?"

"I really don't know, Jennie." A look of apprehension crossed Simon's face. "Many of the others have scattered now that he's here."

"And why didn't you tell me my father was in Silas Ravine?"

Simon's eyes widened. "Why would he go there?"

"For the lode, of course. You have *skills*, just like The Crow. Why didn't you tell me?"

"Who're you talking to?"

She jerked around at Cal's question, who stood to her left. He wasn't in his tent, which explained why she'd heard nothing. She looked back to where Simon had been sitting beside her, but the spot was empty.

"Just mumbling to myself."

The miners labeled them Tommyknockers, but Jennie preferred to call them the *mountain people*. Many a legend had grown around them. She supposed they might be named elf or leprechaun in other places, but she knew them as a race of creatures who co-existed with the mountains and valleys and streams. They were finely tuned to the frequency of the rocks and stones, and were always attracted to the miners who dared to corrupt their home. Many times they helped, but often their mischief caused accidents and tragedy. Jennie had sought to establish a rapport with them when it was clear they liked her but had kept this interaction to herself.

"Where have you been?" she asked.

"Scouting."

"Did you find anything?"

"Maybe." He rested his rifle on his shoulder. "I think you should follow me."

Jennie stood, careful to keep the edges of her duster from getting too close to the fire and climbed behind Cal upwards through a forest of pine trees. She braced her hands on the trunks to keep from slipping. Puffs of breath were visible from her exertions; she shifted her hat so she could look upward to see Cal's broad backside. He waited on a ledge until she reached him, taking her hand to haul her up.

His fingers slowly slipped from hers, the intimacy warm and comforting. Her surprise at the gesture was diverted, however, as her eyes locked on the scene before her.

The large carcass of a bear was spread wide and tall, its arms and legs nailed to trees. Its gut had been slashed, the entrails spilling out.

Tears welled in Jennie's eyes. "Why? Who would do such a thing?"

"Have you ever seen something like this before?" Cal asked, his voice quiet and gentle.

"No." Jennie looked away, swallowing the grief in her throat at so heinous a death.

"It doesn't look recent." Cal rested his left hand on her shoulder and squeezed gently. "But it does appear ritualistic. Any Indian trouble in these parts?"

"Not that I know of. The Utes are fairly peaceful." Jennie glanced back at the animal. "Is that a male or female?"

"I'd say female." Cal removed his hand from her and she immediately missed it.

"Did Augustus do this?" she whispered, swiping at the tears running down her cheeks.

"He doesn't seem terribly ... intelligent. But he's paranoid, and that can make up for much."

"What could this mean?"

His dark gaze watched her—deep pools that seemed to have no end. Simon was right. Cal Boggs trod different pathways than most. "This is meant as a warning and a marker, of sorts. Someone has taken great care to isolate the bear's spirit here."

"Why?"

"Likely to contain what lies ahead."

Alarm snaked through Jennie, and she glanced around. "Are we in trouble?" Her gaze came back to his.

"No. I can protect you."

"Because you're The Crow?"

Cal frowned. "How do you know that?"

The explanation lodged in her throat.

"Who told you, Jennie?" he prodded.

"You won't believe me." She glanced down and wrung her hands.

"Why don't you let me decide about that." His stone-faced expression was at odds with the kindness in his voice.

Should I trust him?

Did she have a choice?

"I can hear the whisper of the peaks and the valleys and the trees. I can understand the streams as they flow through the land." She raised her eyes, defiance giving her strength. "I can speak with the mountain spirits."

As he contemplated her, she waited for him to lecture her about not living in a world of make-believe and fairy tales. But instead, the barest hint of a smile reached his eyes, and he simply gave a slight nod.

In a rush of air, she asked, "You believe me?"

"I do."

A horrific squeal from below filled the air.

"Maisie!" Jennie threw herself from the ledge, tripping as she went and rolling. She quickly stood again and angled herself down the hill as she sought to reach her mule. She side-stepped swiftly along the muddy ground covered in brown pine needles, grabbing at trees to arrest her momentum.

As she came to the spot where the horses and Maisie had been picketed, heaving from her exertions, Cal's strong grip squeezed her upper arm and he pushed past her, his rifle at the ready.

The animals appeared unharmed but whinnied and flicked their heads in agitation. Jennie wished she had her gun. Something, or someone, was no doubt in the vicinity. She edged closer to Cal.

They moved near the animals and Cal made soothing sounds. Jennie placed a hand on Maisie's flank to calm her. A faint bawling came from the bushes. Cal moved toward it, rifle aimed. When he pushed the brush aside with the barrel of his gun, Jennie gasped.

A frightened baby bear watched them.

CHAPTER SIX

I t was mid-afternoon and Cal had only managed to move Jennie, the horses, and Maisie about a mile forward. The bear cub had drastically slowed them down.

He trailed behind Jennie, the cub tucked snuggly against her belly, wrapped in a blanket to calm her. It was a female.

Jennie refused to leave her, having managed to feed the half-starved animal boiled oats. She also got the cub to suckle water from a leather glove with a hole punctured in one of the finger slots.

Cal hadn't thought this was a good idea. He'd tried in vain to convince Jennie to abandon the critter that would likely die anyway. They were simply prolonging the outcome.

"No." Jennie's answer had been firm and unwavering. While Cal respected Jennie's stubbornness, the timing left him frustrated.

"Then take it back to Silverton and I'll continue on alone," he'd responded. "You can describe the location of the ravine to me."

"You can't do this without me." Jennie's pronouncement had slid through his bones, her words implying far more than the search for her father.

He didn't want her to leave.

So he packed up this makeshift family that had come to rely upon him, and they continued their trek. He'd scouted the area in his dreams during the night and knew a cabin sat about two miles ahead. And there were goats. He hadn't appreciated that fact at the time, but now he knew that it might mean milk for the cub.

It was nearly dark when they reached the dwelling. A woman with gray-streaked hair and a stern expression on her bird-like face emerged from the cabin. Immediately the scene appeared odd to Cal, but he couldn't put his finger on it. He wondered if time flowed differently here.

Well-worn timbers hugged the cabin and the roof appeared in need of repair. Gaping holes on the porch hinted at rotting floorboards. The dwelling was sorely in need of upkeep, a pressing concern with winter near.

"Betsy, it's Jennie." Jennie awkwardly swung her leg and dismounted her horse, the cub still bundled against her. He would've helped but didn't want to leave his vantage point as he scouted the cluster of pine trees behind the small homestead.

"Jennie my dear, what a nice surprise." Betsy stepped forward but stopped short when she noticed the bulge in her arms. "Do you have a babe?"

"Of a sort." Jennie carefully pulled back the covering and revealed her treasure.

"Is it a possum?"

Jennie laughed. "No, she's a bear. Her mother was killed. We couldn't leave her." Jennie glanced back at him. "*I* couldn't leave her."

Betsy's gaze landed on Cal. "He your husband?"

"No. That's Cal Boggs. He's helping me look for my father."

"Ben is missing?" Concern crossed Betsy's face.

Jennie nodded.

"Well, come inside, then." Betsy waved them in.

"I'll tend to the animals, ma'am," Cal said.

She nodded curtly but didn't address him directly.

"Would you have any goat milk for the cub?" he asked.

"I've got some. I'll get it for you, Jennie."

Cal wondered at the woman's disdain for him. He'd seen it before.

With the dark features of his Comanche heritage, he looked more Indian than white. And some folks just plain didn't like it.

He saw to the horses and Maisie—unloading the gear, brushing and settling them all in a makeshift shed beside the house. He put out a bucket of oats. There were indeed goats—four in all—along with a pig and several chickens. Betsy surely didn't live alone.

He knocked before entering the cabin as a courtesy. Jennie opened the door, her face flushed and hair disheveled. The bear cub was bawling and rolling around, grabbing items off the table and generally making a ruckus.

"Quickly, come inside!" Jennie demanded, grabbing his arm and pulling him into the cabin then slamming the door. "I don't want her to get away."

"She looks like she's having fun."

Jennie leaned down to scoop up the animal. "I think she's feeling better. She consumed all of Betsy's milk in no time."

Cal enjoyed the happiness on Jennie's face, spellbound for a moment. The cozy intimacy dissolved, however, when he glanced at Betsy, sitting at the table. Her glare was like a cold blast of winter.

Jennie struggled with the bundle in her arms. "We should set up the tents outside. I don't want to disturb Betsy."

Cal raised an eyebrow. "You think you can contain that thing inside canvas walls?"

The bear squirmed and swatted at Jennie's braid, trying to put it into its mouth. "I need you to work with me on this, Cal." She spoke with the tone of an aggrieved mother and Cal felt suitably chastised.

He wanted to question Betsy but sensed that he'd have no luck with it. The older woman had withdrawn to the kitchen area and was busy scrubbing a pot.

Jennie gestured at the table, where a bowl of stew sat. "That's for you."

"Obliged." He sat down and ate as quickly as he could. Jennie added a plate of cornbread and he downed that, as well.

He stood. "Give me a minute to set up the tent, then I'll call you."

"Alright."

Cal erected the accommodations opposite the shed.

When Jennie joined him, the bear cub clung to her waist and snuggled its head against her bosom.

"Can we talk?" he asked.

Jennie indicated her tent. "Can you come inside? I want to get the little one settled."

Cal followed her into the cramped space, a small oil lamp hanging from the tent roof, casting shadows into the eerie night.

"Will you hold her so that I can organize a bed?"

Cal considered the request. The cub opened her eyes and stared at him, the sweetness striking a heartstring. He exhaled deeply. "Yeah, I'll try."

But the little one didn't appreciate the extraction from Jennie, who was forced into close contact with Cal as they tried to enact the transfer. Jennie's hair tickled Cal's nose and his awareness of her hit him full steam. It wouldn't be difficult to bury a hand into the thick strands now in disarray, thanks to the cub.

But he held back.

He hadn't come to Silverton to get tied down by a woman, even one as fetching as Jennie Livingstone.

"Have you given the rascal a name?" he asked, his breath upon the side of Jennie's face.

She glanced up, her face flushed. The cub was now in his arms, so she scooted back. The critter didn't cling to him as it had with Jennie; clearly the soft curves of a human woman were preferable to the hard planes of Cal's body.

"I've just been calling her Little Bear. What do you suggest?"

Taken aback at having his question redirected at him, he paused to consider the request. "In Comanche, a black bear is called *tunayó*."

"We'll call her Tunayó, then." A shy smile tugged at Jennie's mouth.

Gazing into Jennie's forest-green eyes, a deep pull of familiarity encompassed him. Had they known each other in another place and time? His granny had spoken of such things. But even with his dreaming skills, Cal had never believed there was such a woman for him, had never been inclined to peer that closely into his own life.

"Where's Betsy's husband?" he asked.

"She said he's working a claim the next valley over. He should return soon."

The sides of the tent pressed close, a cocoon sheltering them in an intimate embrace. "Has she seen your father?"

"She says she hasn't."

"Do you trust her?"

Her mouth tightened into a grim line. He didn't need her to answer.

Instead, he asked, "Why does she hate Indians?"

Comprehension smoothed the tension from her face. "She survived an Apache attack when she was much younger. I'm ... sorry."

"For what?"

She hesitated. "For her rudeness toward you."

"I'm more concerned about what she might do to *you*."

Jennie gave a slight shake of her head. "Betsy isn't violent. I don't think we have to concern ourselves with that."

"But you think she might know about your father?"

"Maybe. And that bothers me." She turned away and set about unrolling her bedroll and laying blankets upon it. When the task was complete, she settled upon it and held her hands out for the cub, who now dozed in Cal's arms. He deposited the furry bundle into Jennie's arms. She wrapped the creature into a blanket. "Thank you."

The lamplight illuminated Jennie's rosy cheeks and he raised a hand to caress her face, to touch the vitality that pulsed within her. But at the last moment, he swiftly lifted his hat and ran the other hand through his hair to hide the intention.

"I'll be nearby if you need me." He left the tent and went to his own, fumbling around in the dark until he was settled on a pallet.

The connection to Jennie pulsed with lust and yearning and deep knowledge. It vibrated with the longevity of dirt and stone, tree and sky. When he looked into her eyes, he saw a part of himself. What would his

Scottish granny—his *seanmhair*—have said if she still lived? Granny was a *taibhsear*, a seer, much like Callum. There could be no doubt that Cal and his brothers had inherited an affinity for the other world from her. But it was the Comanche that drove them to hunt and track those souls for which evil was second nature. And that was why he was here. To dispatch Harley Jessup, in whatever form the man now existed.

Darkness was at hand, and somehow Jennie's father was in the thick of it.

Cal closed his eyes and sent out an entreaty to his granny. Though she no longer walked the earthly plane, such a request could cross time and space. Steadying his breath, the great need for Jennie lessened, but it never completely left him.

CHAPTER SEVEN

The bear cub awoke Jennie twice during the night. She was prepared the first time with a jar of goat's milk inside the tent; but the second time, she scooped up the bundle of fur and carefully picked her way to Betsy's cabin in the gray haze that preceded sunrise.

Tunayó whined and her mouth sought a teat; Jennie was forced to continually push the critter's face away lest her breasts undergo a painful initiation into motherhood. She let the cub suckle her finger to keep it from waking Betsy.

She went to a small icebox and searched for another jar of milk. She replaced her finger with the leather glove inside the bear's mouth. Although it was empty of liquid, she hoped the activity of suckling would keep the cub occupied. As she located a jar in the storage box, something in the back caught her eye. Unease settled over her.

"What are you doing?"

Jennie jumped at Betsy's voice. "I'm so sorry. I needed more milk for the cub."

"There's a jar in there. Go ahead and take it."

Jennie retrieved it and shut the icebox door, thinking to escape as quickly as she could. But something stopped her. She faced Betsy and noticed how frail the woman was in her nightgown, the dark circles under her eyes and the pallor of her skin.

"What is that in the back of your storage box?" Jennie asked.

Betsy swayed, a bony hand gripping the edge of a chair. "I've got to keep it safe." She raised her other arm and Jennie saw that Betsy's right hand was missing.

Jennie hadn't been mistaken. The appendage was in the icebox.

How had she not noticed it last night?

"Who cut off your hand?" Jennie asked.

"It was Lem."

Jennie shivered despite her thick coat. "Why?"

"He was angry."

"That's terrible." But the vacant look in the older woman's eyes had Jennie slowly moving toward the door.

"It don't matter now. I did what was right."

Jennie stepped to the side, keeping the motion small. "What do you mean?"

"There's lots of whispers in these mountains."

"It's just the wind, Betsy."

"It's the little ones. Lem calls 'em the Knockers." Betsy peered closer at her. "Can you see 'em too?"

"Yes."

"They told me to do it," Betsy continued.

Jennie was nearly to the door. "Do what?"

"They told me to kill those men."

Fear swept through Jennie, shortening her breath. The cub squirmed in her arms. She stole a glance at Tunayó and repositioned the glove back into the critter's mouth. Jennie wondered how quickly she could run out the door.

"Are you talking about the men who disappeared in Silas Ravine?" Jennie whispered.

Betsy paused and Jennie's heart raced so fast she could hear it pounding in her ears.

Jennie didn't want to ask but had to. "Did you kill Ben?"

"Ben? Your pa?" Betsy shook her head. "No."

Relief coursed through Jennie.

"But he was here, and those Knockers wouldn't leave him be."

Catching Betsy in a lie, Jennie responded slowly, "I thought you said you hadn't seen him."

"Did I? You must've misheard me."

Jennie knew she hadn't.

"They whispered in his dreams," Betsy continued. "I could hear it too. They told him they knew of a vein so thick and so sweet that he could never imagine it. He left without even saying goodbye."

"Where did he go?"

"I've no doubt he took himself off to the ravine."

Although Jennie knew this to be true—she had grown to trust Cal, despite only knowing him for a few days—a chill pierced her, nevertheless. She fled outside and sought to steady her nerves.

It was difficult to comprehend that Betsy had killed all those men. The woman must be delusional.

Tunayó's hunger forced Jennie to focus on the cub. By the time the little one was satiated, Jennie's clothes were soaked with goat milk.

Lost in thought, she jumped when Cal appeared. As soon as she saw the grim set of his features, she scrambled to her feet. "What's wrong?"

A brisk wind blew against them, and the cub cuddled closer into her arms. Jennie buried her face into the fur and kissed the animal, stroking the fur to soothe her.

Cal scrubbed his face with a hand. "I really don't know what the hell is going on, but have you seen Betsy this morning?"

"Yes. I just spoke with her."

Shadows danced in Cal's eyes. Leaden skies cast the surroundings in a muted pallor. For the briefest moment, a crow filled her vision as she watched him.

Jennie took a step back.

She blinked, and it was Cal again.

"There's no one here, Jennie." Compassion filled his voice as he delivered the news.

"You mean she's run off?"

"No. By the look of it, this cabin has been vacant for some time."

Jennie pushed past him and ran back into the building, stopping short as she took in the dusty surroundings. She whipped her head around. Everything—the table, chairs, kitchen area and bed—had clearly been unused for weeks, if not months.

"I don't understand," she said. "We spoke with her. She fed us." She glanced down at Tunayó in her arms. "She fed *her*."

From behind, Cal placed both hands on her shoulders. "Spirits cling to places."

"But she was so real. And she wasn't dead. Lem never reported her death. *Someone* would've known. It would've been shared."

She turned to him, and his hands dropped away from her. She immediately missed his touch.

"Maybe everyone only saw her spirit," he said.

"Then why don't we see her anymore?"

"I think it was me. I sent a plea to my granny last night for help."

"Isn't she dead?"

"Yes, but I can still speak with her in dreams. I asked her to clear the way of ... *entities*."

Jennie remembered the icebox. She went to it but the handle wouldn't budge. Cal filled the space behind her and yanked it open. Jennie peered inside.

"What is it?" Cal's voice and presence surrounded her.

Jennie glanced up and was caught in his obsidian gaze. Callum Boggs traveled the shadow places, but the knowledge didn't frighten her. Instead, a yearning ignited, and she wanted to remain close to him. "Betsy's hand is inside."

He reached past her, his shoulder brushing hers. Jennie didn't move. He retrieved a skeletal hand covered with rotting flesh and stared at it.

"Why would that be in there?" Jennie asked.

Cal's dark gaze came to her. "You should go back."

"No. I'm not afraid." She shifted the cub. "Alright, I *am* afraid, but I'm not turning back. I know someone who can help us."

Cal's eyes narrowed. "Who?"

"His name is Simon, and he's a Tommyknocker."

"The little men who bother the miners?"

As sunlight illuminated the cabin, dust danced in the air before Jennie. "Yes. But we can trust Simon. Did your granny purge all the spirits in this area?"

Cal shifted his stance but remained close. "Most likely."

Ignoring the flutter in her stomach from the man before her, Jennie steadied her nerves with a deep breath. The musty odor of the cabin accosted her. "Then we'll need to get out of this place before I can call him."

"What about the cub?"

Jennie looked at him questioningly.

"We can't take her with us," he said.

"We can't leave her. She'll die."

"We don't have enough food."

The goat. If Betsy wasn't real, had the goat been an apparition as well?

Jennie brushed past Cal's stalwart frame and left the cabin, then rounded the corner where the narrow shed stood. There were no animals save for the horses and Maisie. Her heart sank.

A bleating sound filled the air. Jennie spun around as a brown and white goat ran toward her.

Only one, with blessedly engorged teats, but one was all they needed. Jennie knelt and hugged the animal, laughing as it bumped against her face. Tunayó tried to join the fun as well.

Thank you, Betsy.

When Jennie finally brought her attention to Cal, standing just beyond, she froze. "What is it?"

He reluctantly shifted his gaze from her. "Nothing."

But she'd seen it—the wistful longing in his eyes. And she'd sensed the surprise that coursed through him, as if he'd found something completely unexpected. Did she dare hope that *she* was that something?

But she remained with the goat and the cub while he proceeded to take down the tents.

CHAPTER EIGHT

C al guided his horse to a narrow entrance buffered by rocky escarpments, black sentinels in the darkness. He didn't need Jennie to tell him that Silas Ravine lay beyond. A distinct oppressive sensation pushed against him. This place was crawling with ... *something*. He didn't have Kit's ability to *hear* beyond this world, but he didn't need it. His skin prickled with awareness.

He stopped. To go farther with night upon them seemed unwise. While dealing with spirits wasn't beyond his experience, having Jennie with him was a concern. Earlier, watching her with Tunayó and the goat, a protectiveness had filled him, as if he watched *his family*. He couldn't rightly explain his emotions. He'd never desired to settle down before, not even after witnessing his brother Jack fall into an easy repose with Hannah Dobbins. He knew Jack had to love her, heart and soul and then some, because it wasn't in Jack's nature to change his routine for *anyone*. And Cal was much the same.

He dismounted.

"I think this is it," Jennie said.

He gestured to her to hand the cub to him. As he took the bundle of fur from her, Tunayó stirred and tried to climb upward, knocking his hat to the ground and rooting around in his hair.

Jennie laughed and came off her horse. "She likes you."

"I guess I should be glad for the female attention."

"Would you like me to muss your hair as well?"

"I wouldn't stop you."

Jennie's expression became serious. "I've never met anyone like you, Cal Boggs."

The urge to kiss her overtook him, but again he held back. He wanted her, of that there was no doubt, but something told him that if he touched her, he'd never be able to walk away. And in his life, he'd always moved on. "I'm nothing special, Jennie."

As he held Tunayó over his shoulder, Jennie reached up to touch the cub. "I'm not so sure about that. I'm glad you're here with me."

The invitation was clear as she looked up at him. All he had to do was lean forward to capture her mouth with his. He could satisfy his curiosity about what it would be like to taste her, to strip the barriers away between them, to ...

"You take the ragamuffin." He handed the cub to her to break the spell between them. "I'll tend to the animals."

Tunayó gladly jumped into Jennie's arms. Why couldn't Cal do the same?

They made camp and Cal started a fire, thinking it might help to keep all things spooky at bay. As they ate, the horses moved about, unsettled. Cal wondered if any of them would get any sleep tonight.

"Tonight is Hallowtide," Jennie said.

"I know." Cal liked that she used that term instead of Hallowe'en, reminding him of his time with Granny.

Jennie sat across from him, the fire crackling between them. "Simon is afraid of you."

Cal placed a small twig into his mouth. "You can tell him I won't bite."

"He says that crows like to pick out the eyeballs of men."

Cal grinned at the image. "I suppose some do."

"You're not helping."

He poked at the fire. "Alright. You can tell Simon I won't touch his eyeballs."

A short man appeared and sat beside Jennie.

"Cal, this is Simon, my friend."

Cal silently acknowledged the sprite, the dense energy rolling off him in waves. It must take the Tommyknockers a great deal of effort to be seen by humans.

"Is Betsy really dead?" Jennie asked her friend.

"Yep," Simon answered.

"What happened?"

"Her husband and his brother killed her."

"Why?" Cal asked.

"To stop what she was doing in the ravine."

"Is she responsible for all the men who've disappeared?"

Simon nodded.

Cal threw the twig into the fire. "What about Harley Jessup?"

Simon scrunched up his face. "We don't go into the ravine, mostly because of him."

"Is he dead or alive?"

Simon shrugged. "I don't know. We all stay away. I'm sorry I'm not more help. I'm not supposed to talk with you, but I break the rules for Jennie."

"Appreciate it."

Simon leaned forward. "And just so you know, Jennie is special. You'll be sorry if you don't do right by her."

The threat was clear, and Cal wondered if he had competition for Jennie's affections, not that he was in pursuit of them, he reminded himself. "I'll keep that in mind."

"You do that, Mister Crow."

And with that, Simon departed.

"Charming little fella," Cal said. "Why is he so sweet on you?" Damn, but a twinge of jealousy stung him.

"The first time I met Simon, I'd wandered into the most magical patch of evergreens and moss and wildflowers. It felt enchanted to me. I stayed in that place for a long time. It was almost as if I could speak to the rocks and the water and the trees. I suppose that sounds ridiculous."

"No." He was surprised when his voice caught. The picture she painted came vividly to life in Cal's mind, and he couldn't help but imagine lying with her in such a place and loving her.

"Simon said he was drawn to my curiosity."

He wasn't the only one.

Cal sensed the presence of crows in the trees. All of the Boggs brothers could; perhaps this affinity was why they'd picked up the moniker *Crow*. A flock had settled above them—a *molmacha*, as Granny would've called it.

Jennie snuggled Tunayó closer to her, the cub having slept through Simon's visit. "Why are you chasing Harley Jessup? Did he do something personally to you?"

Cal looked at Jennie, her eyes bright with interest, the perfect planes of her nose and cheeks illuminated by firelight. The tug at his sex was sharp and sudden, expanding into his belly and heart and somewhere deep in his chest. *Is this what happens when the soul is captivated?*

Collecting his thoughts, he answered, "No. I've never met Jessup. During the summer, I was passing through Tucson. There's an orphanage in town. I like to stop and visit with the kids when I can. There was a new little girl who'd recently arrived. She'd been passed around from family to family until finally someone had brought her there. She told me how Jessup had taken her family hostage one night. He'd murdered her folks and her brothers. She survived only because when he set a fire, she managed to escape out the back. I knew right then that I'd hunt down that filth and bring justice for that girl's family. So I tracked Jessup to the ravine."

"In your dreams?"

"Yes."

"That's very admirable, Cal."

Tracking Jessup had led him to Jennie. *It must be fate,* distant voices whispered into his ear. Had that little girl led him here not to locate Jessup, but to find something more important?

He knew that he could attempt to scout the future ... *his and Jennie's.* But he wasn't sure he wanted to know. Using his skills to aid on manhunts was one thing, but he had steadfastly refused to explore the intimacy of his own life over the years.

"I think you should try to get some rest," he said.

Jennie silently agreed. Once she and the cub were settled into her tent, he carefully retrieved a wrapped cloth from his saddlebag. Inside, he kept a collection of crow feathers. He chose one and tied it to the entrance of Jennie's tent with a piece of twine.

Beneath his breath, he said, "As night is dark, protect those within. As day is bright, spurn those who seek harm."

When he sensed that Jennie had fallen asleep, the cub with her, Cal slipped into the darkness, his gun and rifle at the ready along with a hatchet and a knife. He moved downwind of the animals so as not to disturb them, entering Silas Ravine alone under the light of a full moon on the night when spirits roamed the earthly plane without restraint.

CHAPTER NINE

J ennie awoke with a start, immediately knowing something was amiss. In the near dark, she searched for Tunayó. When she found no sign of the cub inside the tent, she pulled on her boots, coat, and scarf and scrambled outside.

She searched the area encompassing the camp, startling the horses, Maisie, and the goat but could find no sign of the bear. She ran to Cal's tent.

"Cal, wake up! The cub is gone." She pushed open the entrance and paused, waiting for her eyes to adjust to the inky blackness.

Cal was gone.

Where was he?

Had he taken the cub? It didn't make any sense.

She stepped back and scanned the surroundings. It was still deep in the night, the stars above twinkling in an endless path of lights. Her gaze rested on the entrance to Silas Ravine. They were camped just beside it.

Cal's in there. Despite fear and dread knocking her about, she knew she would need to go after him. But worry gnawed at her over the fate of the cub, so first she continued to search around the tents. If she couldn't locate Tunayó, the little one would never survive.

Finally, she had to accept that the cub wasn't in the area.

Moving swiftly, she entered her tent, grabbed her gun, and slipped a box of cartridges into her coat pocket. As carefully as she could, she crept along the pathway that led into the ravine. Just before entering, she dropped to the ground to inspect it closely.

She found what she was looking for—boot impressions alongside tiny bear prints. The cub had either accompanied Cal or followed him. She supposed the latter. Cal wouldn't have taken Tunayó with him willingly.

She stood.

Caw!

Jumping, she spied a crow in a nearby tree.

Was it Cal?

Her imagination was getting the better of her. Cal couldn't shapeshift into a bird. *Could he?*

Uncertainty pulsed through her, but she moved forward anyway.

As Cal proceeded into the ravine, several crows accompanied him. Their presence didn't calm him. He knew they were drawn to places of imbalance. The land itself could become filled with the energy and echoes of the violence of man, harboring greed and lust and rage, further spurring more horrific acts.

Trees occupied the center of the ravine, but as he climbed higher, he could see in the moonlight that areas had been cleared. The telltale sign of mining—holes dug into the rising cliff sides with the detritus strewn below—showed in many places. Broken down shacks dotted the terrain. He approached one.

He pushed the door aside where it hung askew with the tip of his rifle. Inside were the remains of many bodies stacked on one another, still wearing tattered clothing and reduced mostly to bones.

He left the building and its oppressive atmosphere. The spirits were restless, but nothing that Cal sensed to be dangerous.

An inspection of a second shack unearthed a most peculiar thing. At first, Cal thought it a pile of snakes, but he knew it was too cold for the creatures. A closer look revealed a collection of lariats. From Cal's inquiries, he knew that Harley Jessup had liked his lasso and had owned many. He would often string up a victim with one.

Further inspection confirmed that it was indeed Jessup who'd been here. The tethers had his insignia stamped on the end of each one.

Cal paused. The stillness in the ravine was absolute. Although the crows had followed Cal, they were now silent. He tried to get a sense of Jessup, or perhaps of his spirit.

A sound beyond caught his attention. Cal moved quietly through a stand of pine trees. A man stood up against a larger trunk, his back to Cal. It wasn't Jessup. Cal aimed his gun. "Don't move."

The man started, but slowly raised his arms, a rifle in one hand.

Cal took a step back. "Turn around nice and slow."

Even in the dark, the haggard appearance of the tall man with a graying beard couldn't mask his resemblance to Jennie.

"It's nice to finally meet you, Ben Livingstone."

CHAPTER TEN

"Who're you?"

"A friend." Cal holstered his gun. "I've come here looking for you."

Ben lowered his arms. "How did you know where I was?"

"Lucky guess."

Ben watched Cal with dispassionate eyes.

"Why haven't you returned to Silverton?" Cal asked.

"I can't see what business it is of yours."

"Jennie sent me."

Emotion flared on Ben's face, then was gone. "She's not here, is she?"

Cal didn't answer.

"Shit." Ben shook his head. "You brought her here?"

Despite the heavy coat Ben wore, Cal could see the gauntness of the man's face and frame. "What's goin' on, Ben?"

"First, tell me who you are."

Cal pushed up the edge of his hat. "My name's Cal Boggs. I'm a bounty hunter."

"Is there a bounty on my head?"

"No, sir. Just the wrath of your daughter. But there's another man I'm looking for—Harley Jessup. Seen him around?"

Ben's eyes narrowed. "You must be behind on your fact-gathering. Jessup is dead and has been for some time."

Cal kept his gaze forward while also listening to the sounds of the wilderness beyond. "That's what the townsfolk say."

"But you don't think so?"

"Let's just say I've got an open mind."

Ben smoothed down his unkempt hair and grabbed a hat from the ground, placing it atop his head. "Where's Jennie?"

"Camped outside the ravine."

Ben gave a slight shake of his head. "Goddammit."

"Is she in danger?" Cal held himself back from grabbing Ben by the shirt. "Jessup's not dead, is he?" The edge in his voice brooked no evasion.

Ben nailed him with a steely gaze. "No."

"What the hell are you doing in here, Livingstone?"

"The right thing. Too many men have died or disappeared. The mining prospects can't be ignored. I've had enough of this man and his terror tactics."

"So you came here to deal with it by yourself?"

Ben swallowed convulsively. "It wouldn't leave me be, and no one else would come."

Cal sensed the haze of madness hovering around Ben. "Jennie's worried sick about you."

The man's shoulders dropped. "Yeah, I guess I underestimated her stubbornness."

"You've been here for more than a fortnight," Cal said. "What do you know?"

"Jessup doesn't live in the ravine. He's up on the shoulder above."

Cal glanced in that direction. "Why does he stay here?"

"Can't say, except that the rumors of hauntings have certainly worked in his favor."

"How have you managed to evade him?"

Ben leaned against the tree behind him. "I've been in these hills a long time. I know how to disappear. And it was easier without Jennie tagging along. Why are you hunting him?"

"A promise to a little girl."

"Well, be that as it may, you didn't need to bring *my* little girl here."

"No, sir. But I suspect if I wasn't with her, she would've come alone. At least I was able to look after her."

Ben sized him up, then nodded.

"You best show me where Jessup lives," Cal said. "I'll take care of the rest."

Ben silently agreed.

JENNIE ENTERED THE RAVINE ALONG A TRAIL BARELY VISIBLE THROUGH THE trees and underbrush. She should've brought a lantern, but a sudden shiver made her glad she couldn't be seen in the darkness. Staying undercover, she skirted a hillside, searching for some clue that Cal or Tunayó had been through here.

"Jennie."

She stopped at the sound of her name whispered in her ear and spun around.

It was Simon.

Despite that it was her friend, fear settled in her bones. She wanted to ask him what she should do but couldn't find the words.

"He's dead, Jennie."

Her mind raced. *Who?*

"You need to be careful."

Simon disappeared.

Who did he mean? Her papa? Cal?

Frantic, she turned in circles, trying to decide what she should do, then froze as a large shadow grew before her. Trembling, she stumbled back, never taking her eyes from the creature.

Suddenly, strong arms grabbed her from behind. "Don't move." Her heart sank from the unrecognizable voice. The man's putrid breath heated the skin behind her ear. "It's a bear."

"Let go of me." She yanked one arm from him, taking care to keep her movements small. She didn't want to set the bear off.

He chuckled. "A lot of men have come in here, but never many women. Just Betsy. And now, you."

Looking over her shoulder, she glanced at the man. Wide, beady eyes watched her from above a mustached mouth, the thick ends hanging to his chin. "You must be Harley Jessup," she whispered.

A loud snort from the adult bear redirected her attention forward.

"Yep." He chuckled from behind her. "It's difficult being so famous."

A side glance showed him to have a rifle. "Are you going to shoot the bear?"

Jennie jumped as the animal let out a bellow.

Harley sighed. "Well, I hate to waste a bullet. I know this bear. She's been in these parts as long as I have. She recently lost a cub, and that's left her grief-stricken and angry. I'll just let her take *you*."

Jennie's eyes darted from side to side, searching for some way out. Tunayó could be the mama bear's babe, and Jennie was certain the cub was in the ravine. She just needed to find her. Surely that would appease the adult bear's bad temper.

But Jennie knew there was no hope. Even if she could outrun the giant beast, the human beast beside her wasn't going to let her live.

It was warmer in the ravine, and a mist had settled around them. In a rush of commotion, a flock of crows swooped among the trees, crying and screaming. Jennie covered her ears but knew it was her only chance. She ran and didn't look back.

CHAPTER ELEVEN

A s a cacophony of screeching crows split the silence of the dark night, Cal bolted from Ben's side and ran back into the ravine. The call of the ebony birds guided him. Unable to see beyond several yards as he dropped into the tree line due to the fog, he unleashed his instincts, borne of Comanche might and Scottish temperament.

He caught the man by surprise, slamming him into the ground. Although his adversary fought back, Cal's strength easily overpowered him. He hooked his arm around the man's neck and pulled his Colt, cocking the hammer and pointing the barrel at the man's temple.

Ben emerged from the mist, breathing heavily. "That's not Jessup. It's Lem Atkins."

JENNIE RAN UPWARD INTO A CLEARING THEN DOWNHILL PAST A WOODEN building. She stumbled into a thicket of underbrush and prayed she wasn't followed. She slowed and chanced her first glance behind her. Thankfully, no man or bear followed. She folded herself into the shadows and fog, ears alert for signs. The distant sound of the cawing crows could still be heard, but closer, a bawling swirled along the night air. She moved carefully toward it, finally reaching the source.

Tunayó.

Jennie gratefully scooped up the bundle.

Now, to find the mama bear.

"HARLEY JESSUP IS DEAD." WIDE-EYED, LEM ATKINS'S GAZE DARTED between Cal and Ben from where they all sat on boulders hidden in the forest.

"No, he's not." Ben's face took on a grim line as he adjusted his floppy hat. "I've been in this ravine for over ten days now, and I've seen him many times."

"You've seen his ghost."

Cal thought of Betsy and knew that Lem might be correct. "How did your wife die, Mister Atkins?" Cal asked. "Wasn't her name Betsy?"

Lem hesitated.

"Betsy's dead?" Ben asked, nailing Cal with a shocked gaze that he soon shifted to Lem.

"She is. And Lem knows it. Who cut her hand off?"

Lem swallowed and flexed his jaw. Even in the dark the grime covering the man's face was visible while the pungent odor of his unbathed body rolled off him in waves, nearly choking Cal.

"Did you kill your wife, Lem?" Cal asked.

"I had to." His voice was barely a whisper. "She killed all those men. She was gonna kill me, and Augustus. We had no choice."

Ben stood. "Betsy killed the men who've disappeared up here? But Jessup's here. Surely, he did it."

Lem glanced around nervously. "Look, I don't claim to know how this all works, with the living and the dead taking residence in the same place. Betsy was never right after Jessup appeared in these hills and died. I don't know if she was possessed of him, 'cuz that just sounds so crazy. But there's no getting around how strange it is here. I didn't know what she was doin' at first, then Augustus and I began to suspect. I feared for my life."

Ben loomed over Atkins. "Why didn't you tell the marshal in Silverton?"

"*You* hardly believe me. What would he have said?"

"Did you sacrifice that bear down in the valley?" Cal asked.

"Augustus did it. He learned of spells and such from the Ute. He used it to rid the spirits." He shook his head. "But it ain't workin'."

Cal inhaled sharply. "No, it's not."

"It's Hallowe'en tonight, and it's always bad on this night."

Cal scanned around them, the area still cloaked in fog. "Then why are you here?"

"Because I thought I should move Betsy's body. Augustus and I dumped her in a mine shaft and I've never felt right about it since. Maybe if I put her to proper rest, she'll leave me be."

"She still lives with you at your cabin?"

Lem released a ragged breath. "Yep. I stay away as much as I can, but my nerves can't take much more of it." He lowered his voice. "She follows me."

"I can help you with your wife, but first I need *your* help. Harley Jessup needs to leave this earth, once and for all."

Lem shored himself up. "Alright, whatta you want me to do?"

CHAPTER TWELVE

Jennie found herself in a thicket. She could hardly see before her so moved slowly, clutching Tunayó to her, the cub nestled against her, clinging and agitated. As she inched forward, her foot caught and she tumbled. The cub was pulled from her arms as she rolled. She came to rest hard against a tree trunk, stunned.

Lying on her back, she winced when she tried to move. Above her, a starry sky peeked through the treetops. Slowly, an object fluttered toward her from above, spinning and twirling, until it softly landed upon her nose. She reached up to examine it.

A black feather.

A crow's feather.

Jennie wondered over the oddity of it landing right on her face.

A shadow blocked the twinkling stars and Jennie repressed a gasp as a large snout loomed above her.

Mama bear.

How had she not heard the animal's approach?

The musky scent of fur assaulted Jennie's nose as the large beast huffed in rapid succession. With a pounding heart, Jennie tried not to move, *not to breathe*. If she was motionless, maybe the bear would leave her be.

Jennie squeezed her eyes shut, praying she wasn't about to be gutted. *Please, please, please.*

The bear swung its head back and forth but stopped as the bawling cub approached. Tunayó clambered onto Jennie's torso, but Jennie restrained herself from handling the animal. She lay as still as she could, as if she were already dead.

The mama bear huffed and snorted loudly as Tunayó began to bawl. Jennie watched it all through slitted eyes, struggling to breathe as the heavy cub sat atop her chest.

Finally, the mother bear turned to leave. Tunayó leaned over and licked Jennie's face.

"I love you too, little one," Jennie whispered. "But you need to go with your mama."

The cub clambered off of her and ran to catch up to its mother.

Jennie listened—unmoving—as the two of them disappeared into the night.

As sad as she was to say goodbye to Tunayó, she couldn't believe her luck in not being attacked by the mother.

She sat upright and pulled sticks and leaves from her hair.

Beyond, she saw Simon, along with at least twenty additional mountain people, all male from the look of it. She'd never encountered so many Tommyknockers in one place. "I thought you all didn't come here."

"We've made an exception," Simon replied. "We've come to help you."

"Did you just save me from the bear?"

"No. You seem to have the protection of The Crow."

Jennie stood, remembering the black feather, but it was lost now on the ground. "Can you help me find Cal and my father?"

"Yes. Everyone is in agreement this one time. We'll help you."

CAL WAITED IN THE WOODS WITH BEN AND LEM. SOON, BETSY APPEARED, summoned by her husband. She didn't acknowledge any of the men but moved past them—as impenetrable a manifestation as when he'd seen her the previous night. It was uncanny how real she looked.

Cal pulled his Colt and retrieved a stone from his shirt pocket. He needed to prepare for a physical encounter, but he knew it could just as likely be a supernatural one. He rarely used the stone, but the gift from his granny—Bonnie Boggs—was meant for just such a conflict as this. It had come from the Forest of Rothiemurchus, in the Highlands of Scotland, a place strongly tied to the otherworld. Most men couldn't handle the *touch*, but as Granny liked to say, "Ach, my grandsons aren't most men." The forest carried the spirit of Seath Mor, a great warrior of long ago and Chief of the Clan Shaw. Through Cal, the stone would amplify the great chief's spirit and channel the man's strength.

The mist cleared and a half-moon now hung in the sky above, offering illumination to the surroundings. A man entered from the shadows and was greeted by Betsy. Cal didn't need confirmation to know that it was Harley Jessup.

The gathering happened quickly—Ben and Lem to Cal's right, a large huffing black bear and cub behind Jessup and Betsy, and the sudden appearance of Jennie with a band of short men. Cal held his surprise in check as his eyes met hers. The brief look of elation on her face was directed solely at him, warming him through. Then her eyes found her papa's, and Cal shook his head to keep her from running to her father. He hoped the little mountain men would keep her safe.

Then the crows came, a *molmacha* filled with dozens of birds. Their ear-splitting cries echoed throughout the ravine, with a cacophony of rattles and clicks interspersed. But as they settled onto the tree branches above, they became eerily quiet.

Cal focused on Jessup. The man was as solid as Betsy, and Cal could full well understand why Ben thought the man still lived. But now that Cal was in his presence there was no mistaking it—Harley Jessup was good and dead.

"Time to move on," Cal said.

Jessup cocked his head. "Who're you?"

"I'm cleaning up loose ends. You don't belong here. If you weren't dead already, I'd take care of that for the deeds you've done."

Jessup chuckled. "I ain't dead."

"I don't really care what you think. I made a promise to a little girl, and I intend to keep it."

"Sure is a lot people here tonight." Harley swung his gaze to Jennie. "You ran off, sweetheart."

The man's hungry interest in Jennie sent a surge of alarm through Cal. The crows came to life and dropped from the trees, swarming the group. Ben, Lem, and Jennie all fell to the ground, but Cal remained standing, grasping the stone in his hand as a tingling energy flowed from it.

Harley Jessup never stood a chance.

The crows opened a doorway and Cal sent Jessup through it, then he dropped the scorching rock to the ground.

With Jessup gone, the heavy oppression in the air evaporated.

"I guess he really was dead," Ben muttered from where he'd crouched. "Jennie!"

But Jennie was gone.

"Where is she?" Cal asked the mountain men, who all gaped at what had just occurred.

"She was here a minute ago," Simon said. "The crows frightened us."

"Where's Betsy?"

Lem took off running. "She's gone to the mine shaft."

Cal retrieved the stone, then he and Ben followed in great haste.

CHAPTER THIRTEEN

Jennie tried to stop herself, but an unseen force propelled her forward.

Betsy moved alongside. "I can't help you now, Jennie."

"I don't understand." Jennie tripped but was compelled to stand and run. She thought to pull the gun from her coat pocket, but she knew bullets wouldn't work on the woman.

They stopped at the edge of a chasm and Jennie screamed, balancing so as not to fall from the side. She clung to a nearby rock, fearing that Betsy meant to throw her over.

Betsy peered over the side. "That's where Lem left me."

"I'm so sorry. I wish we could've helped you." Her foot slid and she struggled to keep hold of the boulder.

"Harley Jessup wasn't so bad. He was just trying to protect this area for himself. I killed those men to help him."

"I'm sure you thought you were doing the right thing."

"You don't understand what it's like out here."

Jennie clambered to find a hand hold. "I do, Betsy. I do. It's very lonely, isn't it?"

"You live with the animals, and then you become one."

Jennie's tenuous hold on the only anchor she could find ceased to be effective. She was about to slip from the side. "Betsy, please help me!"

The old woman simply watched her.

Jennie shrieked as the ground began to shift beneath her. She desperately grabbed at anything that would keep her from falling, trying to brace herself with her feet. A hand seized hers just as the ground fell away.

Cal!

He hauled her up and, holding her close, took her away from the edge. Jennie embraced him, shaking. When she looked up, she saw his stoic face, blanched with fear.

"I thought I was going to lose you," he whispered.

Without thinking, she kissed him. His stiff response didn't deter her; she pulled him closer and fully slanted her lips over his.

"Jennie!" Her papa's voice broke the spell and Cal released her, his face unreadable. Had she been wrong about what lay between them?

She went to her father and hugged him. "I'm glad you're alright, Papa."

"What happened?" Ben asked, releasing her.

Lem knelt by the edge of the drop-off. "Is she gone?"

"Yes," Cal replied.

Lem looked up at him. "Did you cause that earthquake?"

Jennie caught sight of Simon, who said, "No, that was us."

But none of the men appeared to see him.

"That was a stupid move," Cal said. Apparently, he could hear Simon.

"Causing the tremor?" Lem asked, not realizing that Cal spoke to the Tommyknocker.

"You could've killed Jennie." Cal barely contained his anger.

Hope flared in her heart. *Maybe he does care.* The taste of him lingered on her lips.

"It wasn't me." Lem stood, prepared to argue with Cal.

"I'm not talking to you," Cal said. "There's a Knocker here."

"They're real?"

"Yes," Jennie answered. "Thank you, Simon, for trying to help."

"Sorry we botched it up," the mountain sprite replied. "It's a good thing The Crow is looking out for you. I think you're in good hands."

Jennie didn't answer, afraid she'd embarrass herself in front of Cal.

"The others have left," Simon continued, "so I'm off too. Farewell, Jennie. See you in the hills."

"Goodbye, Simon."

Her father swung his gaze to her. "Who is Simon?"

"It's a long story, Papa. Can we just go home? Then, I'll tell you all about it."

Ben placed an arm around his daughter's shoulder. "Alright. I'll leave this place, but I plan to return. Lem, I'll be filing a claim on the vein with the assayer. I can include you in it."

Lem nodded. "Yep. I think it might be time to try again here." He turned to Cal. "Are you gonna take me in for the murder of my wife?"

In the moonlight, Cal's dark hair shone like the body of a crow. "No. I'd say you suffered enough. Before I leave, I'll let the marshal know it was an accident. You helped me get Jessup. I'd say we're all even now."

"I'm indebted to you," Lem said.

"Where will you go now?" Jennie asked Cal, unable to stop herself, the sensation of him slipping away hitting her full force.

"I expect I'll go see my brother, Jack. His daughter was born on this night."

"How do you know?"

A smile graced his lips, not unlike the one he'd gifted her with on the day he offered to take her into the ravine. "I know."

Was it possible to ask him to stay? Would he even consider it? How could she entice a crow to remain?

A knot formed in her stomach. A man like Callum Boggs, who straddled the divide between the living and the dead, surely would find domesticity far too confining to consider.

Sadness enveloped Jennie. It was clear her life would never be the same without him.

CHAPTER FOURTEEN

C al awoke from the dream and stared at the flowered wallpaper, visible in the moonlight shining through the window. The room at the Silverton Hotel was small and clean, and he'd accepted that this was his refuge for the last night in this town. He planned to leave on the train in the morning.

But the dream cloaked him like the warm embrace of a lover.

Jennie.

He wanted her, but it wasn't in his nature to stay. Anywhere.

But the vision had been clear—two children, a boy and a girl, and they both resembled Jennie too much for him to doubt they were hers.

And his.

When Jennie kissed him at the ravine, the connection had shot clear to his toes. It had taken everything he had not to respond to her. He wanted to crawl into the darkness with her and never leave. But they'd had an audience, and Cal wasn't one to lose control over a woman.

During the return trek to Silverton, Cal had done his best to put the bone-deep connection he felt for Jennie aside. It was for the best. He'd depart the next morning, moving on like he always had. He wasn't suited for settling down, and Jennie deserved better.

He was The Crow—bounty hunter, gunfighter, a Highland warrior who pulsed with Comanche blood. He faced down death and chased evil as a matter of course. But the love of one woman left him angst-ridden.

Jack had settled down. When he'd found Hannah, he didn't hesitate.

So why am I uncertain?

The dream couldn't be denied. He sat upright in bed and scrubbed a hand over his face, scratching at the stubble on his cheeks.

The thought of leaving Jennie behind was gnawing a hole in his gut, alongside a persistent arousal. He'd never before denied himself the pursuit of a woman if she was interested—and Jennie had made it abundantly clear she was—and it was near driving him mad.

Callum Boggs, you'll never find another like her. His granny's voice filled his head. *She's a Livingstone. Her ancestors came from Scotland, as well. She was destined for you.*

A soft tap on his door caught him by surprise.

He stood, wrapping a blanket around his waist to cover his nakedness, and waited. The tapping came again. It couldn't possibly be Jennie, yet he hoped. He'd certainly not given her any reason to come to him.

He opened the door and there she stood, eyes wide and face glowing. She struggled to catch her breath, as if she'd run here. Her eyes dropped to his bare torso, and she licked her lips. Excitement coursed through him. He was such an idiot to think he could leave her.

"Just tell me one thing," she said. "Do you like me, Callum Boggs?"

He grabbed her hand, pulled her into the room, and shut the door. He captured her mouth with his, tasting her, then deepened the kiss, letting her know just *how much* he liked her. The blanket dropped to the floor, but she didn't hesitate, didn't withdraw. Wrapping his arms around her, he brought her against the length of his body.

Hunger for her pressed on him with such need that he pushed the heavy coat from her shoulders as her hands explored his chest and stomach, arousing him further. She helped him remove her boots, shirt, and trousers then he guided her to the edge of the bed, laying her back, baring her to him. Her soft curves, always hidden beneath layers of clothing, beckoned—and he explored the luscious bounty with his mouth.

But he had little time before his patience failed him. Bracing himself over her, he kissed her as his body joined with hers. He was her first, and he forced himself to pause. "I'm sorry if I've hurt you," he whispered.

"No." She buried her hands in his hair, her breathing frantic, and bent her knees to allow him deeper access. "Don't stop."

His body shuddered. With a primal need he took Jennie; she clung to him, matching his rhythm with her own increasing need, and in the release, the ancient connection revealed itself. Jennie was his. His heart had always belonged to her.

In the aftermath, still reeling from the encounter, he raised himself above her to look into her exquisite face. "Why did you come here tonight?"

A serene and satiated expression crossed her face. "I dreamt of you, and when I awoke, a crow was tapping on my window. I had to see you. I had to try and convince you to stay."

He nuzzled her neck, inhaling the scent of this woman—*his woman*—that reminded him of the heather-capped Highland fields. It occurred to him that Silverton wasn't so different than the Scotland of his heritage.

He ran a hand along the curves beneath him. "I tried to leave, but even before you came here, I knew I wouldn't be able to."

"Then my convincing has seemed to work."

He continued to love her until the sun rose.

CHAPTER FIFTEEN

Six Months Later

Winter finally broke and the town of Silverton enjoyed sunshine and warmth on the first day of May.

Cal knew exactly where his wife was headed, so planted himself at the bottom of the stairs of their small two-story home, located down the street from Ben Livingstone. He drank coffee and read yesterday's copy of the *La Plata Miner*.

When Jennie descended a short time later, she placed her hands on her hips when she came to where he sat on the bottom step, blocking her passage.

He glanced up at her. Forced to wear loose skirts due to her expanding waistline, he enjoyed the more feminine look.

She arched an eyebrow. "Is there a reason you're not sitting at the kitchen table?"

He stood, his face level with his beautiful bride, and enjoyed the flash of annoyance in her emerald eyes. "Because I know what you're thinking, and the answer is no."

She pursed her lips, briefly distracting him as he recalled loving that mouth—and much more—during the night. "I'm only five months along and finally feeling better. It's not a long ride to Silas

Ravine. I'd be with Papa. You know I'm curious as to the state of the mining now that the valleys have opened up after the winter thaw."

Cal place a hand on her abdomen and the child within. *My son.* Jennie and the babe had fast become the center of his world.

"Will you at least wait a few days?" he asked. "Then I can take you."

He'd traded manhunting for carpentry and was currently working on a renovation of the San Juan Restaurant and Bakery.

Letting out a frustrated moan, Jennie leaned forward and kissed him, lingering against his lips. "Fine. I'll wait for you." She swatted his hand as he tried to unbutton her blouse.

He chuckled.

"I should've listened to Simon," she added. *"Cha bhi sinn 'g a innseadh do na feannagan."*

We won't tell the crows.

"You're Gaelic is improving, but The Crow always knows."

"You didn't know about me." Her expression became serious. "I'm glad you stayed."

He brought a hand to her cheek and stroked her chin with his thumb. "I love you, Jennie."

The home of his heart smiled. "And I love you, Crow."

A MURDER OF CROWS

Eliza McCulloch is determined to reclaim her family book of spells and her only hope is Kester Boggs, a manhunter called The Crow.

CHAPTER ONE

Arizona Territory
October 1878

K it Boggs downed the last of his rye whiskey and settled into
the wooden chair, the supports creaking loudly. He fully
expected the contraption to give out at any time. He usually kept his
liquor intake to a minimum when on a hunt, but the firewater was so
watered down that he indulged his thirst.

From his vantage point outside the Wild Dog Cantina, the midday
bustle of La Noria buzzed like a bee's nest. The border town—strad-
dling Mexico and the Arizona Territory—was occupied by mostly
local white and Hispanic farmers, but the streets were also swarming
with the hungry and savage looks of men who had arrived in search
of work in the nearby Patagonia Mountains. With their eyes clouded
with dreams of riches, these desperados were no doubt intent on
striking it big with copper or silver. But that wasn't what had brought
Kit so far south, farther than the usual region he and his manhunting
brothers patrolled.

As he watched the main street, his gaze was drawn to a woman
riding a lathered red Indian pony. Both exhibited a stubborn bearing.
The woman stopped before the mercantile and slid from the horse,

tying the reins to the hitching post, her clothing covered in dust and the hem of her skirt frayed. Pausing, she removed her hat and wiped sweat from her forehead. She gripped the wooden support and appeared to take a fortifying breath, then leaned her head back to read the overhead sign. Her dark hair spilled down her back, loosened from the pins of the bun at the base of her neck, and Kit's eyes were drawn to the outline of her feminine curves.

"Kester Boggs?"

Reluctantly, Boggs turned to the scrawny Mexican beside him. "Nobody uses that." He planted all four legs of the chair to the ground. "Call me Kit."

"Like a kitten?" The gaunt man was also missing a few teeth.

"No." Kit's voice was resolute. "Do you have news for me?"

"*Sí*. They will see you tomorrow in an abandoned smithy at the far end of town."

"What time?"

"Ten o'clock."

"*Gracias.*" Kit tossed a coin at the man, then turned back to the woman. She was gone.

Damn.

He searched up and down the street for her horse, but both animal and female were nowhere in sight.

Had he imagined her?

He leaned forward and adjusted his Stetson. He'd been on a cat-and-mouse game these past few months and his reserves were pushed to the limit. Manhunts were his repertoire, but he usually had his brothers with him. Jack, however, had slipped headfirst into the arms of Hannah Dobbin, swiftly losing his edge for bounties since he wanted to remain near his new wife and the impending birth of their first babe—due any day now. And Callum had ventured to Colorado, speaking cryptically of a dream he'd had and the need to investigate. Kit had been ready to accompany him when rumors that Hamish Kerr was spotted down south had reached Kit's ears. There had been little time to waste.

Now that a seed had been planted in La Noria, Kit would see if it paid off tomorrow.

He scanned the street once more. The disheveled siren was good and gone. Just as well. It was best not to get distracted.

It was bad enough that no voices from the other realms whispered in his ear, since it was those very voices that often gave Kit the edge he needed in his work. This only added to the strangeness of the town— calm on the surface with an undercurrent of cutthroat.

And the wind carried a whiff of desperate survival, along with a stench of stone-cold fear.

Surely, the dead inhabited this place as much as the living. Kerr couldn't be far, since a man as vile as he had most assuredly made a deal with the Devil. It was said he kept company with *El Viejo del Saco* —also called The Bag Man due to the *criatura's* propensity to appear before children as an old man with a sack over his shoulder. It was this demon that Kit was determined to find and vanquish, this monster that preyed on the blood of the young.

Maybe the mysterious woman wasn't of this world, either. Perhaps the Maker had sent her mirage to soothe Kit's ragged and exhausted thoughts.

He rose and left the cantina, going directly to the tiny room he had rented at a dilapidated boardinghouse. Despite daylight still working hard to take the late October chill from the air, Kit shed his clothing and fell into a deep sleep.

He dreamt of the siren.

———

ELIZA McCULLOCH PEEKED AROUND THE ADOBE BUILDING. ALL CLEAR. She moved along the darkened alleyway, careful to make little noise. When she had arrived in town earlier, she'd thought to march straight into the mercantile and ask where Hamish Kerr lived, but instead, she'd caught sight of the ruddy-faced man she suspected had been trailing her since Tucson. She'd quickly grabbed her horse's reins and blended into a nearby crowd.

She had spent the last three weeks making her way from her home in Taos, and while she'd occasionally encountered men of crass manners, it had been nothing of true concern. But this one was different. Her extra sense—the McCulloch gift—had signaled something was amiss.

And not just with the man following her.

She'd felt something as she stood outside the mercantile. Could the McCulloch Grimoire be inside? It was outlandish that it might be so, but she hadn't wanted to wait until morning to find out.

Hamish Kerr had stolen her family book of spells over twenty years ago. If it was now sitting in a dry goods store in this god-forsaken location on the Mexican frontier, then didn't she have a right to it? Setting aside the fact she would be breaking the law, Eliza had concocted a plan as she'd waited for night to fall: She would steal it.

The grimoire was a book woven with the history and magic of the Shaw clan, created by her Scottish grandmother, Beitiris Shaw McCulloch. It had belonged to Eliza's mother, Marta, along with Marta's two sisters before Hamish had taken it.

While Eliza regretted trespassing in the mercantile, the sooner she found the grimoire, the sooner she could return it to her mother. And perhaps it would aid in finding her cousins—Deirdre and Catriona.

Her mama and her aunts—Aileen and Rose—didn't know she was here. They didn't know that Eliza had overheard them discussing the theft of the book by a man named Hamish Kerr; they didn't know that she'd eavesdropped on their growing concern that Dee and Cat hadn't been heard from these past two months after a trip from the McCulloch home to Tucson.

Eliza crept to the mercantile now bathed in black shadows. It was three a.m., the best time to do a little sleuthing. She reached for the door and found it locked. Hardly a surprise, but it was worth checking first.

Her eyes shifted to the window.

She glanced around. Not a soul was in sight.

Before she could talk herself out of trespassing, she stepped to the pane, wrapped the edge of her skirt around her right hand, and punched hard into the glass, wincing from the sound of the window shattering as well as the impact. She continued to knock jagged pieces away to clear the opening as best she could, then she wiggled into the store, the fabric of her already worn-out dress tearing further. She suppressed a grunt as protruding shards scratched her torso, and slivers penetrated her hands.

She landed on the floor with a thud, knocking into a table filled with canisters of coffee which crashed in a cacophony of sound.

She stood and whipped her head around, searching for anyone who might be present. But she was alone. As she silently gasped for air, she brushed debris from her skirt, fragments of glass bloodying her palms. Ignoring the discomfort, she searched for books among the modest supplies of goods. When she found several volumes on a low shelf, she squinted in the darkness as she struggled to read the titles. She hadn't even been born when the grimoire had been stolen, so she really had no idea as to its appearance. But her mother and aunts had crafted a second grimoire over the years; unfortunately, it was inferior to the original. Beitiris—Granny Bea in all the tales handed down to Eliza, Dee, and Cat—had had a skill in the natural arts that none of the women had been able to match. Still, Marta had often remarked that Eliza was a spitting image of the old woman.

Perhaps the new grimoire resembled the old. Eliza searched for a match.

When she clasped the final tomb of the collection, her heartbeat quickened, her fingers tingled, and her forehead perspired despite the brisk night air pouring in through the broken window.

She knew before she opened the cover that this was it.

Careful not to stain the tome with her bloodied hands, she opened the book. On the title page was an inscription. She cursed not bringing a light, but had she used a candle it might have alerted someone to her presence. Or worse, she might have accidentally caught the book on fire. Too risky.

She moved to the window and held the book up to the moonlight that offered slightly better illumination. The words were in Scottish

Gaelic. Thanks to her mother and aunts, Eliza was well-versed in the language of her ancestors.

A 'nighean mar a mathair.

Such mother, such daughter.

Or, as Aunt Rose liked to say, *Like mother, like daughter.* It was an oft used phrase of Eliza's upbringing.

Exiting through the window, she clutched the book to her bosom and swiftly ran down an alleyway beside the building. Abruptly she halted, fear surging through her.

A shadow shifted.

She stood unmoving. Eliza couldn't take her eyes from the form that slowly appeared.

She blinked, not believing what she saw.

A three-headed dog. And a large one at that, with its trio of fangs bared.

Taking a step back, she prepared to flee but bumped into something. A man? It was the last thing she remembered.

CHAPTER TWO

K it entered the abandoned smithy late morning the next day, dust motes floating in the slanting sunlight. Once again, the spirits were silent.

Never in Kit's life had *nothing* whispered in his ear.

Three men stood in a far corner, hidden in the gloom.

The tallest, his face pock-marked, spoke. "We are told you wish to see Hamish Kerr."

"That's right."

"For what purpose?"

Kit did a quick scan of the weapons the men bore, a pistol on each hip. "I have news."

"Of what?"

"A pending delivery of orphaned children."

"Where?"

Kit shook his head. "No. I'll only speak to Kerr."

"Why on earth should we believe you?"

As Kit raised a hand to his collar, the men opposite him immediately reacted by resting their palms on the butt of their guns.

"Easy," Kit said. "I just want to show you something." He pulled down his shirt enough to reveal his lower neck and the symbol that had been branded onto him by the Comanche.

The man with the nightmarish face leaned forward, his gaze calculating. "You have the mark of the crow." He grimaced. "You are one of *them*."

"Who?" the man to the right asked.

"It is said there are a band of crows—disguised as men in the light of day—that hunt in the dark places."

It was a tale that had been spread by Kit himself, along with Callum and Jack. It often made their work easier using their reputation to flush out the ilk they sought, saving them unnecessary bloodshed. In this case, however, Kit was forced to dangle blood—and that of children, no less—to get Kerr's attention. It soured his stomach. He would get *El Viejo del Saco* if it was the last thing he did. And to do it, he needed to get close to Hamish Kerr.

The tall man paused, then nodded. "I will take you to Hamish. Tomorrow. Be ready at dawn. It's a full day's journey."

"To where?" Kit asked.

"You don't need to know that. But as a gesture of our good faith, we invite you to dine with us this evening. And there will be a surprise."

"I don't like surprises," Kit said.

"Then you can say no. We'll expect you at Maria's Place at seven."

"And who should I ask for?"

Mottle-face grinned. "You can call me Johnny. And I'll call you …?"

"Kit Boggs."

A shine flashed in Johnny's eyes. "The Crow," he whispered.

CHAPTER THREE

L ater that evening, after a meal of charred meat and undercooked beans, Johnny brought Kit into a room with four women standing in a row, their gazes vacant. It was obvious, even without the chatter of the dead, that these women's spirits had left their bodies.

Kit strained for a whisper, for anything that would alert him to what was really happening, but again there was nothing but silence from the other realm. It was obvious why Johnny had brought him here—Kit was to choose a companion for the night. The idea turned his stomach even more, if that was possible, after dealing with Johnny and his gang.

Kit entertained the idea of demanding all four so that he could free the females, but at this point, such a move would simply draw undue attention to himself.

One of the women shifted her stance and a fifth female became visible, standing hidden in a corner. Her hands were tied behind her and her mouth was gagged. Her barely clad bosom heaved up and down as she sucked in breath after breath, her eyes wide, flashing with fear and anger. Her spirit was fully intact.

The siren.

When Kit's eyes met hers, heat flamed in his chest, shot into his arms and legs, and consumed his skin like fire ants. Stunned, he waited while the effect slowly dissipated.

What the hell was that?

He dragged his gaze back to the others, but his choice was clear.

"Choose one," Johnny said. "A gift for you on this blustery night."

Kit looked at each woman in turn. The first four wouldn't meet his eyes, but when he got to the siren, she narrowed her gaze and pinned him with a steely resolve. He certainly had no intention of using any woman tonight, but it was obvious this wildcat was sure he would.

"I'll take her," he said.

Surprise registered on her face, quickly replaced with apprehension.

Johnny nodded. "Interesting choice. I thought she might suit you. She's new, but if she gives you any trouble, be sure to let us know. When you're done, the others"—he gave a nod to his men—"will want a shot at her. We'll bring her to your room shortly."

Kit departed before he did something stupid like untie her and reassure her that she would be safe with him. As to the other women, he vowed he would try to help them when this was all over. If he was still standing.

He returned to his room and waited.

A pounding on the door rattled the hinges. Kit swung it open, and immediately he sensed the panic emanating from the siren. *His siren.*

He gave a nod and stood aside so she could enter his room. Her captor, one of Johnny's men, shoved her so hard that she stumbled. Kit shot an arm out to prevent her from falling.

"Easy," he murmured.

She was a slight thing, and it took little effort to stand her upright.

"*Gracias,*" Kit said, his voice edged with anger. There was nothing grateful in his response, except that at least the woman would be safe from Johnny's men. For now.

The man grinned, then chuckled. "You're the first to touch her. Good luck, *amigo.*"

Kit didn't respond. He slammed the door in the man's face, then turned to the woman. She was glancing all around the room and backing up in the process, trying to put as much distance between them as possible. Kit knew his appearance must frighten her. He was tall, with thick black hair that fell to his shoulders, and while he had Scottish ancestry on his pa's side, his mother had been Comanche, and he had the look of her people.

"I won't hurt you," he said.

The woman snapped her eyes to him, wariness dancing in their depths.

"You can stay here tonight," he added.

She tensed.

He held up a hand. "You don't have to lie with me. But you'll have to let the others think you did, and all night long, unless you want me to send you back to that snake pit. I doubt the others will be as accommodating as me."

She simply stared and didn't speak.

He moved closer, and she took another step back.

"I'm just gonna remove the rag," he said, raising his hand slowly. He carefully pulled the dirty bandanna free of her mouth. "What's your name?"

More silence.

"You're not chatty," he said. "I like you already."

He leaned down and pulled a knife from his boot. When she saw it, she stumbled backward until the wall stopped her.

He sighed. "You don't need to be so skittish. I told you I wouldn't hurt you. I just want to remove the rope around your hands."

He stepped close. She'd backed herself to a narrow spot between a table and the bed. She refused to give him any latitude to get behind her, so he was forced to lean close, wrapping his arms around her to hook his small blade into the hemp binding her wrists.

He tried to ignore her skin, dewy from perspiration, and the brush of breasts that were covered by a thin blouse, the edges of a tattered undergarment visible. She had the smell of fear, but beneath it was a smoky, earthy aroma, like that of a campfire.

He sliced through the rope, letting the binding drop to the floor, and stepped away from her. As she rubbed her wrists, her gaze locked on him. To avoid her scrutiny—and to get his reaction to her under control—he focused on returning the knife to his boot.

She was no whore, despite Johnny and his men treating her as such.

"You can take the bed." He motioned toward it. "You look like you could use a rest. Are you hungry?"

She gave one slight shake of her head. Elation filled him that he'd managed to get a response from her. At this rate, he ought to have her name by next week.

She watched him with wide eyes, rubbing her arms as if she were holding herself upright, then slowly sat down on the edge of the bed across from him.

"You expect me to believe that I'm not your entertainment for the night?" Her voice was low and rich, warming him like that campfire she had so recently sat beside.

The small room closed in around him, and he was acutely aware that he found her far too compelling.

Needing a distraction, he pulled his Colt and began inspecting it. "I'm not needing company."

"You don't prefer women?" Her question sliced through the thick atmosphere that had been building between them, but Kit thought he heard the faintest tone of curiosity in her voice.

He raised his eyes to hers. "I don't prefer *unwilling* women." He held her gaze until she fidgeted. He allowed a slight smile to tug at his mouth.

"Where are you from?" he asked.

"North."

She was American. He rolled the barrel. Full. "You got a name?"

"Do you?"

His gun was in order. It always was. This was a ridiculous exercise. He holstered the weapon again, craving a bit of whiskey to settle his nerves. But if he drank, she would probably cower from him again. And he didn't want her to.

"Kester Boggs. But you can call me Kit." He leaned forward and rested his forearms on his knees. When she didn't respond, he glanced up.

She was frozen again, staring at him.

Her eyes narrowed and she said, "Boggs, you say?"

"Do I know you?"

Rather than answer his question, she said, "Did your family come from Scotland?"

He gave a nod. "On my father's side."

Her attention sharpened the longer she watched him. "Where in Scotland?"

"The Highlands."

She shook her head, as if in some argument with herself, her expression no longer one of fear. It was as if she had just learned a secret. "I'm Eliza McCulloch."

McCulloch?

"I can see by your expression that you're acquainted with my family name. Yes, I'm one of *those* McCulloch's."

During his childhood, Kit's granny had offered up plenty of warnings about the dangers of creatures on the *other* side, along with the men who would make unholy bargains with the darker forces on earth, but there had only been one admonishment when it came to his Scottish heritage: *Stay away from McCulloch women.*

To be honest, he'd never paid much attention to the warning. As far as he could remember, the McCullochs lived in Scotland. Kit and his brothers had grown up in Missouri, and now called the western territories their domain. A warning such as that was so far beyond his world that he'd paid it little thought.

Until now.

What was the history between the Boggs and McCulloch families? Searching his memory, he came up empty-handed. Was Granny turning over in her grave? He cocked his ear, wondering if she'd whisper what he wanted to know. But she had been a quiet spirit during the fourteen years since her death, never once conversing with him. Perhaps it was the distance. While she and his gramps had stayed for a time in

Missouri with Kit, his brothers, and his folks, she had returned to Scotland three years before her death, finding her resting place in the land of sprites and faeries. Kit was grateful that he and his family had sailed with her and Gramps to visit the land that Bonnie Boggs had so loved.

"Are you sufficiently repulsed by my presence?" she asked, her demeanor changing from fearful to more confident with each passing moment.

Hardly. Had his granny simply thought McCulloch women too homely for Boggs men? If that were true, she was off by a mile. Eliza McCulloch possessed an allure far beyond any other female he'd been acquainted with.

Siren.

Was that the reason he and his brothers were to avoid females of this lineage? If only he could remember.

"Why are you here?" he asked.

She took a deep breath, which only served to draw his gaze to her shapely attributes. For a wild moment, he wondered if she would succumb if he tried to seduce her. But he'd promised her safety from the appetites of men.

"I'm looking for a man called Hamish Kerr."

Get in line.

"It wasn't wise to come here alone," Kit said. "It didn't take long for the locals to nab you."

"Yes, that was unfortunate. I plan to be more careful."

Was it his imagination, or was there more color in Miss McCulloch's cheeks, more strength in her body as she sat straighter, more determination in eyes previously clouded with trepidation and confusion?

"Did they drug you?" he asked.

"I believe so. I won't be caught unaware again." Her warning hung in the air.

Witch.

The word echoed in his ear. *Granny? Are you finally going to talk to me?*

"But perhaps Fate is lending a hand and brought me to you," Eliza continued. "The men who took me spoke of you. They called you The Crow. Why?"

He shrugged. "It's just a name that my brothers and I are called."

Should he tell her that they hunted bounties for a living, chasing the depraved and *otherworldly* criminals that most normal manhunters avoided? Why was he even considering an admission of his livelihood to a woman he was supposed to avoid?

In the span of a few short minutes, her face had begun animating from stone-cold statue into a living, breathing woman, and she was nothing short of breathtaking.

Stray thoughts of wooing her bounded forward like a stampede of horses.

What the hell is happening?

When Jack found Hannah, Kit couldn't deny it had started him thinking, and damn if settling down hadn't been crossing his mind of late. Frustrated by his train of thought, he wished he had another gun to inspect if only to divert his thoughts, but he'd only brought the Colt. He had stashed his bow and arrow at the livery—he hadn't wanted to arrive to Hamish Kerr's posse with too much weaponry in hand.

"There are more of you?" she asked.

He gave a nod. "But I'm currently alone."

"Would you help me, Mister Crow?"

"Like I said, you can call me Kit. Why are you looking for Kerr?"

"Unfinished business."

"Why would you get into bed with a Boggs?" He immediately regretted his choice of words, not only from the withering look Eliza cast upon him, but also because bedding her was a desire that had taken residence in his head, and he doubted it would leave anytime soon.

A Boggs is never to touch a McCulloch.

Kit set his jaw. It was definitely Granny in his ear. Hell of a time for her suddenly to confide in him. He bristled at the smug authority in her tone, transporting him back to his boyhood when Granny's exasperation with him inevitably led to one of her rantings.

"Kester, your stubbornness will lead you into trouble. I'm trying to help you. It's my duty to teach you. Heed my warning, grandson."

"I'm not offering you my body, Crow," Eliza said, an edge to her words.

"What *are* you offering?"

"You're a hunter of the night. I'll pay you to help me track down Hamish Kerr."

Leaning back in the chair, Kit stretched out his legs and crossed them at the ankle. He almost laughed. This whole thing was going south, and fast. As much as he'd like to help the pretty McCulloch, she had no business going anywhere near Hamish.

"I'm afraid I've got my own agenda," he answered. "You should let this go, and you should leave town as soon as possible."

Eliza arched an eyebrow. "Let me get this straight. You tell me I'm incapable of handling this myself, but when I ask for your help, you say no." She shook her head, her look dismissive. "Then, I will leave." She stood.

He immediately came to his feet, blocking her path to the door. "No."

"You don't want to bed me, and you don't want to help me. I think we're done here."

How wrong she was on the first count, but he didn't voice it aloud.

"Get out of my way," she demanded. "I'll find Kerr on my own."

It would seem he wasn't about to be free of the McCulloch siren after all. And despite the danger, a traitorous part of him was glad for it.

Kit brought his hand to her dark hair and lifted the strands spilling over her shoulder. The awareness between them was palpable. It pleased him that she didn't pull away.

"Fine." He watched her, but she wouldn't meet his eyes. "I'll help you."

"A McCulloch cannot bind herself to a Boggs," she whispered, then raised her gaze, renewed once again with a flash of hard determination. "I offered to pay you, not to pleasure you."

He didn't bother to hide his grin, which soon turned into a full-on laugh.

CHAPTER FOUR

E liza awoke with a start. Kester Boggs—the man called The Crow —was gone, leaving her alone in his room. She sat up and pushed the woolen blanket aside, having slept in her clothing.

How had a McCulloch never crossed paths with a Boggs until now?

Avoiding a Boggs man had always been part of family lore. Eliza's recollection of the warning was filled with accusations of dark magic spanning centuries. Granny Bea had warned her daughters—Aileen, Rose, and Marta—to never become entangled with a Boggs man. Each of them in turn had imparted the same warning to their own daughters—Deirdre, Catriona, and Eliza. Surely the details were in the McCulloch Grimoire, which Eliza had briefly possessed before encountering that unholy beast in the darkened La Noria alleyway.

And where was the book now?

She had to assume that Johnny—the foul-looking man who had been trailing her since Tucson—and his disgusting compadres had it, and they would likely alert Hamish that Eliza had stolen it. It was clear that Kerr ran this town.

Would it be returned to the mercantile? Since she had found it there in the first place, it was obviously of little value to anyone, least of all Hamish, so if she could just slip away from Boggs she could check the store again.

Eliza shoved her feet into her boots and laced them tight, wincing from the cuts on her hand. She adjusted her blouse, annoyed by the tears in the material.

Mister Boggs had agreed to help her find Hamish Kerr, but if she could locate the grimoire again, she wouldn't need that aid after all. Because while Boggs had been true to his word and hadn't touched her, perhaps he would eventually tire of his chivalry and rescind that promise.

But that didn't ring true.

As a child, she'd imagined a Boggs to have yellow eyes and horns sprouting from his head, but the one who'd saved her from Johnny's gang wasn't anything close to that description.

Kester Boggs was tall, with broad shoulders and hair the color of night, and he wasn't unpleasant to cast eyes upon. At all. It was quite the opposite. He was handsome in a way that made her curious about him.

She shook off the thought.

This must be why McCulloch women were warned away from Boggs men. They possessed a charm that could be used for ill gains and evil ways. That had to be it.

She considered weaving a spell, but for that she would need her belongings and they were with her horse, which was stashed at the livery. The vile men had nabbed and drugged her, likely with laudanum, and it had impeded her ability to defend herself. She supposed she should be grateful that Boggs had rescued her, but she immediately scolded herself.

Boggs didn't rescue me. He's simply waiting for the right time to get what he wants.

And what would a man like that want with a woman such as herself? A woman he acquired as nothing more than a prisoner?

The obvious, of course.

Eliza would never let a man abuse her in such a way. The scars her mother bore—both seen and unseen—had made Eliza acutely aware of what a man could do to a woman.

The door opened, startling Eliza, and Mister Boggs entered. He tossed a pile of clothing at her. "Put this on."

She quickly sorted through it—a sturdier blouse and skirt, and new undergarments. "Thank you." It was a kind gesture, considering the tattered state of her current clothing.

His gaze lingered on her, and she felt his interest as clearly as if he had touched her. Kester Boggs did want her.

A flash of warmth bloomed in her face and shot straight to her toes.

Why did she feel a sense of victory? Why did a part of her wonder what would happen if she agreed to the desire in his eyes?

Ambivalence held her rooted in place. She waited for Kester Boggs to be like all men, because surely he was like *all men*. But her woman's sense, her witch's sense, strummed a tune that said he wasn't.

"I'll be back in an hour," he said. He pulled his Colt and held it out to her.

She stared at his hand, stunned. "What are you doing?"

"Do you know you to use it?"

"Yes." She'd taught herself how to shoot. Her cousins had had little interest in learning about weapons, believing their other skills would keep them safe, but Eliza had always hedged all her bets. It was why she was willing to enter into an agreement with The Crow.

"Take it."

She grabbed hold of the gun.

"If someone other than me comes in, then shoot."

Was he seriously giving her his weapon? "But it's the only gun you have."

"No."

"What if I shoot *you*?"

"Sweetheart, you need to make up your mind. You're not my prisoner. But if you're about to go with me into the wilds to find Hamish, then you need to accept that I'm not your enemy." Amusement glittered in his eyes. "At least, not yet."

She froze. Was that a threat?

He grinned. "Relax. I'm just worried that one of Johnny's men might stop in for a visit. At least this will give you a fighting chance." He turned to leave, then looked back at her. "But try not to hurt yourself. I'll come back for you."

He left the room and shut the door, and emptiness echoed around her. Eliza stood rooted in place, the gun heavy in her hand.

A twinge plucked at her heart. A softening. A tenderness. For a Boggs.

For Kester Boggs.

She refocused her determination and quickly changed her clothes, slipping the gun into a skirt pocket. She had just enough time to visit the mercantile and search for the grimoire. Unfortunately, it wasn't there.

Eliza quickly returned to the room she had shared with The Crow and waited for him. It was an entirely practical and prudent move, she told herself. He would help her find Hamish Kerr. Never mind that she waited for his return like a lovesick puppy.

KIT REINED HIS HORSE TO A STOP AND RAISED THE COLLAR OF HIS DUSTER to ward off the whistling wind. It was late afternoon and Johnny had stopped his horse just ahead, along with six other men.

A glance over his shoulder confirmed that Eliza still trailed behind on her Indian pony, her pink cheeks visible despite the scarf wrapped around her head. When he'd come back for her, she'd still been there. Kit hadn't been certain she wouldn't flee, but he'd been glad.

He shouldn't be. Eliza was a loose end he didn't need. A complication.

She'd had gear stashed at the livery with her horse, and Kit had helped her retrieve it before they'd set off toward the Patagonia Mountains with Johnny and his men, supposedly headed to Hamish. Or so they said.

"We must walk from here," Johnny said. He and his men dismounted.

Kit swung from his horse, then moved to Eliza. He'd had to tie her hands to make good on the charade that she was nothing more than chattel to him, while casually insisting that he wanted to keep her for a time before handing her back to Johnny and his gang. Johnny had acquiesced with a speculative gleam in his eye that continued to nag at Kit.

He helped her from her animal, ignoring the feel of her despite the gloves on his hands and the thick wool jacket she wore. He didn't want to convey any type of attachment. Not that he *was* attached to her, dammit.

A McCulloch can't bind herself to a Boggs.

"Apparently a McCulloch *can* be bound by a Boggs," he remarked under his breath, tugging at the hemp around her wrists.

He smiled at the flash of displeasure in her eyes.

She pinched her lips. "Don't push your luck, Boggs."

"I'm not." The binding was too tight, so he started to loosen it, blocking the view with his body so that Johnny or any of his men wouldn't see what he was doing. "Just looking forward to the payment you'll owe me."

"That's only if we find Kerr."

Once the rope wasn't so tight, he knotted it again, leaving it loose so she could easily slip free if needed.

"Thank you," she said, her voice low, reluctant.

"If we don't find Kerr, you'll still owe me for this protection."

He eyes snapped to his, her expression wary.

He gave a slight shake of his head. "That's not what I meant. You've no need to be frightened. You can repay me by telling me of the feud between our families."

"You don't know?"

"Well, I was a boy when Granny Boggs instilled the fear of God into me and my brothers about a McCulloch woman. I'll admit I wasn't paying much attention. I never really thought to face one of you heathens from the underworld."

She swore softly under her breath, so he gifted her with a reprimanding stare.

She scoffed. "The saintly look doesn't become you, Kester. You're probably King of the Underworld himself."

"No. I think that's reserved for the likes of Hamish Kerr."

Eliza stared at him, seeming to agree. "I suppose the Boggs-McCulloch feud seems very far from the time and place where it started. Have you ever even been to Scotland?"

"Once, when I was a boy."

"You're lucky. I've never visited." She glanced at him and took a step back, her expression a bit bashful.

He had crowded her, but it had been to keep their conservation private. "Maybe one day you will."

Up close, her skin was pale and soft, her lips rosy, and her eyes pools of green, like the forests of the Highlands.

She gave a nod and a bit of a smile. "When this is over, I'll tell you why we are never to ... fraternize."

"Then I shall consider myself paid in full."

"Let's go!" Johnny shouted.

Kit turned and entered the mountains, dark clouds above them, a chill wind howling, and night coming. As they descended into the bowels of the earth, it was only fitting that today was All Hallow's Eve.

CHAPTER FIVE

The sky released a deluge of rain. Eliza followed Kit, who led both of their horses. Johnny had insisted she be tethered to one of the men, and Kit had made sure she was bound to none but him.

The Crow wasn't anything as she had expected of a Boggs man.

But now, with the unrelenting downpour, he was a typical male, making no effort to stop and take shelter. Instead, the trail had turned to mud, and they continued to slog onward. Eliza couldn't make out much of anything except for Boggs ahead of her.

Occasionally, he waited for her to close the gap that kept widening between them, but once she reached his position, he simply continued trudging forward.

Try as she might, she couldn't deny that having his company offered her a sliver of comfort, because she was, after all, a prisoner. The darkness and conditions began to press in on her.

Kit lifted his hat and placed it onto her head since hers was long lost. She acknowledged him with a nod of gratitude, a cascade of water streaming off the edge instead of directly onto her. She was still miserable and cold, but it was a small improvement, and she would take it.

Without warning, water began to rise around her boots, the ground now saturated. To her mounting terror, they stood in a quickly building flood. She glanced around but could see nothing in the pitch black. As the rain ricocheted off Kit's hat, the horses snorted in agitation.

She took a step and slipped, falling to her knees. Before she could stand, a wave slammed into her. Flailing, she flew down the hillside, trying to grab hold of something. *Anything.* Water blasted down her nose and throat, and she fought for air but there was none.

She was drowning.

KIT HELD TIGHT TO THE REINS OF THE HORSES AS A COLUMN OF WATER HIT them. He scrambled to the right to gain higher ground, dragging the panicked animals with him.

Eliza was nowhere to be found.

"Eliza! Eliza!"

Having found a perch where he and the horses could stand, he left them and slid back to Eliza's location just moments ago.

She was gone.

He moved farther down the hillside, sliding through the muck and current.

"Eliza!"

In a flash, the crows descended, a cacophony of cawing filling his ears despite the roar of the storm. Where to send them?

A darker mass filled the sky, dipping and changing in size.

Bats.

The crows followed. Kit blended with the corvids, his senses their senses, his sight their sight. He saw her, tumbling in the torrent of water rushing down the hill. As one, the flock of birds swooped in, their claws grabbing her clothing, the mass lifting her from the rushing cascade and bringing her back to Kit. As they released Eliza, he caught her in his arms, sending both of them tumbling onto the muddy ground. He rolled from atop her and helped her to her hands and knees. Coughing, she hacked out water then sucked in loud gulps of air.

The rain stopped as suddenly as it had begun.

Kit clasped her hand and brought her to stand. She'd lost his hat and they were both covered in mud.

Her chest heaved as she pushed wet hair from her eyes. "You have the ability to call upon the crows?"

"That was my first time." He wiped water from his eyes. While the birds often shadowed him and his brothers, he had never purposefully summoned a flock, or a *molmacha* as his granny liked to call them. "But I wouldn't have known where to find you without the bats."

"My familiar. I would guess the crow is yours."

Johnny appeared, speaking to them as if nothing had just happened. "You two need to pick up the pace. We need to get out of this valley before the moon sits above us."

Once Johnny walked away, Kit grabbed hold of Eliza's hand and led her forward, determined not to lose her again.

At last Johnny stopped, and Eliza was heartily glad. Despite that Kit had put her atop her pony, the wet and cold had sapped her energy. She was exhausted.

"We will rest only a very short time," Johnny said.

Everyone began to unpack saddle bags and bedrolls from their horses, settling themselves to the ground, which was oddly not very sodden. In a stupor, Eliza didn't move. She tried to focus her thoughts, but they flew from her mind much like the white puffs of her breath in the chilled night air.

Then Kit was at her side, and his strong hands lifted her from the saddle to the ground. She wobbled, and he held her upright. "Let me make a fire to get you warm."

She leaned into him. Without any warning, a fierce carnal desire blazed to life, and every female part of her—from breasts to womb—craved satisfaction. From him. The Crow. *A Boggs man.*

She squeezed his arms and caught his gaze as she barely

suppressed the urge to hungrily consume his mouth with hers. His eyes were hard, unrelenting, but there was no doubt in her mind that he knew what was happening to her.

A beastly growl caused Eliza to jump and spin around. Kit stepped in front of her, his gun unholstered and at the ready. She swallowed against the panic building in her chest while her body still hummed with need for The Crow.

Peering into the darkness, she waited for the predator to pounce.

The bright full moon fully crested the horizon, and the outline of a large cat became visible. Two yellow eyes flashed as the creature turned its focus more fully toward them.

"Mountain lion," she whispered.

Kit took a step back and bumped into her. Heedless of ancient family warnings, she clung to him. Kit Boggs flowed through her veins, and she suddenly feared for his life.

She had to help him.

The cat lowered its head, its shoulders tense, its haunches appearing to be spring-loaded.

Eliza uttered the spell under her breath.

> *"The moon is bright,*
> *The stars alight.*
> *The rock will quake,*
> *When the spirits awake.*
> *I offer up this sacred vow,*
> *Turn this creature, here and now."*

The mountain lion stepped back, shook its head, and then yawned wide. With no sound, it dashed away into the shadows forming beneath the pearly light of moonbeam.

She stared in shock.

She had cast that spell three times in the past year, and it had never worked. She'd spoken it now because she'd been unable to think of anything else. The achievement filled her with a flush of pride, and she almost giggled over the outcome. Grateful that it had worked, she couldn't help but wonder how. And why now? She was hardly at her best, either physically or mentally.

Kit looked over his shoulder at her and it was only then she realized she still gripped his arm tightly with both hands. Reluctantly, she loosened her hold while some reckless side of her imagined stripping him naked and exploring every inch of his body.

She caught his gaze, unreadable in the darkness, but the hard lines of his cheeks were visible.

"How did you do that?" he asked.

She fully released his arm and said, "You didn't think 'McCulloch Witch' was just a rumor, did you?"

Johnny moved beside them, a soft glow emanating from his eyes, but when Eliza looked again, it was gone.

He grunted, the sound conveying both surprise and derision. "Lucky cusses. The devil cat never turns when she's picked her prey."

With her fatigue dissipated, Eliza extended her awareness outward to touch the senses of the bat colony nearby, the ones who had already helped her. They confirmed the cat had fled. In her heightened state she could feel Boggs, his essence a low but steady pulse. She probed further. When she caught a flash of desire, she stopped and pulled back.

Embarrassed by her curiosity, she released a breath to gather herself.

Boggs was as drawn to her as she was to him. Why would this be? Was he the Devil in disguise? Was she nothing more than a helpless fly drawn to his false nectar?

"The panther has fled," Eliza said.

Johnny had crossed the camp to sit and rest, but Eliza still felt his eyes on her. Perhaps Kit did, as well, since he said nothing more. The men settled to a spot on the ground, and Eliza did the same. Her weariness soon returned. Trusting that the bats guarded the perimeter —at least for now—Eliza fell into a quick but deep sleep.

She dreamt of crows.

CHAPTER SIX

K it awoke to fire.

He bolted to his feet. The camp was surrounded by a wall of flame.

In a frantic search, he found Eliza on the ground, coughing. He pulled her to stand and held tight, folding her into his arms to shield her from the heat. He scanned for an escape route.

They were alone; Johnny and the others were nowhere to be seen. Kit brought an arm up to block the smoke from his face while his other arm kept Eliza pinned to him.

Suspicion filled his head, but he pushed it aside. He would make sure Eliza was safe first, and then he would confront Johnny.

He opened himself to the whispers of the dead, despite that they'd been quiet on this journey thus far.

"I need a way out," he said aloud.

"The fire has sealed the boundary," Eliza said, her voice muffled against his chest.

She'd misunderstood, assuming Kit was speaking to her, but she was right. They stood in the center of a ring of flames and wouldn't last much longer; it was getting more difficult to breathe the longer he waited.

Then came a clear and booming voice, stronger than any connection Kit had ever had in the spirit realm.

I am The Horseman. Do not ignore the power of the McCulloch lineage. You have always been tied to her.

Kit looked down at Eliza. "Can you help us?"

Bewilderment marred her features.

Let her protect you.

"Can you mark a different boundary?" Kit asked.

Her confusion yielded to a dawning realization. She knelt to the ground and quickly traced two large triangles, one atop the other, forming a pentagram.

She came to her feet and yanked him toward her. "Stand inside."

There was just enough room for the two of them to occupy the center of the five-pointed star. Kit pressed her curves against him once more.

"Now what?" he asked.

Craning her neck, her face was so close he could feel her breath on his lips. "We pray," she said.

Would they survive? If this was his end, then he had nothing to lose.

His mouth covered hers, consuming her with an unrelenting hunger that he'd kept clamped down from the moment he'd spied her on the dusty streets of La Noria.

She matched him, returning his kiss with greedy desperation before tearing her mouth from his and burying her face into his chest once again.

The blaze grew higher, closing in with fiery ferocity, and Kit tried to cover Eliza's body with his hands and arms, shielding her. The fire was inches from his face, but still, they didn't burn.

He reached out his fingers and felt a barrier, an invisible shield, protecting them from flame, heat, and smoke.

"What did you do?" he asked.

"We're in another place, maybe even another time."

"How?"

But she didn't answer his question.

Kit couldn't say how long they remained entwined as he resisted the urge to kiss her again, but images cascaded into his mind—dark-haired girls laughing in merriment and a stoic boy the spitting image of Eliza; a ranch house in the green mountains of Colorado, wood stacked outside, smoke spiraling from the chimney; a corral holding horses and a pen containing pigs. Beside the house was a garden and a woman working in the dirt. She wiped a hand on her brow, stood, and smiled. *Eliza.*

The fire had died to embers, and Kit reluctantly released the witch who had saved him. She glanced at him, her face filled with shock.

Had she shared his vision?

"It makes no sense," she said.

But Kit was beginning to think that it did. Pivoting, he kept Eliza behind him as Johnny materialized.

"Enough with the tests," Kit said. The fire had simply been too much. "Show yourself, Hamish."

Johnny laughed. "Excellent." His ruddy features gave way to a smoother complexion, giving him a youthful look. Instead of the drunken, disheveled appearance he'd presented, his gaze became clear-eyed and calculating.

Eliza gasped and tried to push past Kit, but he thrust an arm out and stopped her.

"Why?" Kit asked.

Hamish narrowed his gaze. "I was curious about you two. I wanted to see what would happen if you mingled your gifts."

Eliza managed to step around Kit anyway. "You took something from my mother and aunts, and I want it back."

"The grimoire." Hamish nodded. "I've had my eye on you, Eliza. You can have the book." He waved his hand dismissively. "It's been useless to me, anyway. Come with me." He turned and left them, the remaining men no longer around.

Eliza began to follow so Kit halted her progress once again. "I'm not certain you should go."

"I came for the grimoire. I'm not leaving without it."

"You're risking your life for a book?"

"Not just any book. It was the original collection of spells and family rituals compiled by my Granny Bea—Beitiris Shaw McCulloch. It's a family treasure that Hamish stole from my mother."

"Fine. I'll get your damned book while you high-tail it back to town."

"No." Her eyes flashed with defiance. "I won't let you follow that man alone."

"He's no man. And neither is that which keeps company with him."

"Then all the more reason for me to help you."

"Eliza, I don't need your help," he said, his voice laced with frustration.

"And I don't need you seducing me, confusing my thoughts, and my body ... and ... and ..."

"That's not what's happening."

"It's been a long journey to find Hamish Kerr," she hissed in a low whisper. "I'm not running away now. And I will not be bullied by the likes of you. Get out of my way, Boggs." She pushed past him.

Kit followed, struggling to keep pace with her.

He reached out to his granny but there was no response.

The spirits had been too quiet since Kit had been in La Noria and had been especially so whenever he'd been around Johnny. But it had been Hamish all along. That would certainly explain it.

Although one spirit had been loud and clear.

"Do you know The Horseman?" he asked Eliza.

She looked back at him but kept walking. "Why?"

"Is he on our side?"

She didn't hesitate. "Yes."

He was forced to slow down to grab the horse's reins, and Eliza increased the distance between them.

Kit hoped she was right because he feared they were walking into a trap.

CHAPTER SEVEN

E liza followed Hamish into a darkened tunnel. Kit had tethered the horses at the cave entrance and trailed behind her. They were forced to stay close because Hamish had connected a rope between them. Bringing up the rear were the men that had been part of Hamish's gang when he was presenting himself as Johnny. They had reappeared after the fire.

Apprehension ran an icy finger along her spine, igniting gooseflesh from head to toe.

Could she handle Hamish?

When she'd overheard her mother and aunts discussing the missing grimoire, it hadn't occurred to Eliza that Hamish might be possessed of *gifts*. At least, nothing of merit. With growing dread, she was beginning to wonder if she had miscalculated her goal.

And what of The Crow?

Her attraction to the man was a damned nuisance.

It surprised her that her spell with the mountain lion had worked. She was even more shocked that the pentagram barrier had protected her and Boggs. It was as if something had drawn and focused her intention. Had it been Boggs? Did he somehow enhance her ability to do magic? Was this the true reason for the warning between their families?

The tunnel angled downward, and Eliza sensed they were entering the bowels of the earth. The chilled air outside had given way to a humid and warmer climate, although now that they were dropping in elevation, a damp coolness was present.

Hamish held a torch, and the flickering light caused shadows to dance along the walls. Eliza's gaze kept sliding to them, imagining they performed some macabre ritual.

While her mother and aunts had given her and her cousins a thorough education in the natural arts, in the energies that coexist with humans in this dimension, she had little experience with dark entities. Was that what Hamish was?

Looking over her shoulder Kit's features had blended into the darkness and she caught a glimpse of his true nature, a crow's long beak and black eyes watching her. She blinked, and Kit was back.

Unsettled, she snapped her gaze forward, focusing on the rock-strewn and uneven path of the mining tunnel.

They arrived at a large cavern, slowly illuminated as the accompanying men lit several torches along the walls, a draft drawing the smoke upward. A stone altar stood at the center. As Eliza scanned the area, her eyes landed on a far corner with iron cages. A heap of something lay at the bottom of both.

No!

She bolted toward it, yanking the line that had her bound to Boggs, dragging him with her.

"Dee! Cat!" Her voice shook as she dropped to her knees. She clasped the bars with both hands, her wrists tied together, and shook the doorway of the prison, trying to open it.

Dee stirred, opening her eyes. "Eliza," she whispered. "You shouldn't have come."

Eliza threaded her fingers through the metal slats and grabbed Dee's outstretched hand. Her cousin was filthy, with matted red hair, and a strong smell of waste and despair accosted Eliza. "I'm going to get you out of here," she whispered.

A spark of life ignited in Dee's amber eyes. "Be careful." She shifted her gaze over Eliza's shoulder. "Who is that?"

Eliza could feel Kit behind her. "He's here to help."

Inside the adjacent cage, Cat had pushed herself to a sitting position. Her pale face—so like Dee's that they were often mistaken for sisters—was streaked with dirt. Her eyes were also fixed on The Crow.

Boggs clasped Eliza's arm with his bound hands and forced her to stand. One of Hamish's men pushed them to the stone altar.

Hamish faced her. "A reunion with your sisters can wait."

"They're my cousins," she said before thinking.

Hamish smiled. "No. They're your sisters."

She didn't respond, not wanting to give him the satisfaction of a response but she had no idea what he was talking about.

"Didn't your mother ever tell you?" Hamish asked, raising an eyebrow. "*I'm* your father."

"That's not true." Surely, he would lie about anything.

"Didn't Marta tell you that I took your family grimoire? Isn't that why you traveled all this way?"

Eliza didn't answer.

"Did she fail to mention that it was I who had lain with each of the McCulloch women?" He smirked and revealed a slice of the nasty man beneath the handsome face. "I bedded each of them—Aileen and Rose, and I saved Marta for last. They each produced a child." He raised an eyebrow in triumph. "*My* child."

Dread filled Eliza. Was it true? Why hadn't her mother ever told her?

"And why didn't you know, you're asking," Hamish said, as if reading her mind. "Honestly, I'm a little surprised, even hurt, that none of my paramours ever mentioned me to you girls. But, I suppose, perhaps they regretted the union. I made sure I planted a child in the womb of each."

"Why?" It was clear now that the scars her mama and aunts bore had come from this man. Eliza's heart broke for them. "Why would you do such a thing?"

Hamish's face twisted, and his eyes flashed with anger. Eliza flinched when an explosion snapped from his fingers. "Because I need you girls, my daughters, to help me. I've waited a long time for this."

He stepped close and stared at her. "Those two"—he flicked his head toward the cages—"have proven themselves less than worthy, so I've pinned all my hopes on you." He smiled, but it looked more like a sneer.

Despite the rancid odor of his breath, Eliza held her ground. She needed to keep her wits about her if she had any hope of escape.

"And what, exactly, would you have me do?" she asked, glad her voice remained calm.

Hamish stepped back, a pleased expression smoothing his features. He flicked a glance at Kit. "Open a portal to The Horseman."

The Horseman? "Why?"

"The why is none of your business. Your sisters failed. I won't have use for any of you if *you* fail." He pinned her with a glare. "So don't fail. I believe you have an advantage over your sisters. You have *him*." Hamish's eyes slid to Kit again. "One of the infamous Crow manhunters. There were never any orphans, were there?" he asked Kit. "I knew you weren't dealing in the blood of youth, but I had a hunch that you could perhaps light a fire under little Eliza, being a witch like her feckless mother. Nothing like mixing a Boggs and a McCulloch." He beamed with delight.

Eliza watched Kit, and it was like looking into an endless void. A frisson of fear tickled the back of her neck. Was Boggs even human? She swayed, dizzy from the implication.

She had always taken pride in her skills, in her ability to weave and work the energies of nature. The fearful called it witchcraft, but Eliza knew that it was a skill available to anyone. Most people were simply never taught The Way, so most never believed. And what was misunderstood was so often labeled evil.

Eliza steadied herself. Among the McCulloch women, she had one ability the others did not. She could open pathways to the other side. With this skill, she had always been able to summon The Horseman, a guide from beyond. For the past three hundred years, he'd been a protector to her family.

"What does Boggs have to do with me?" Eliza asked, but her body hummed enough when she was around him that if the mood were lighter, she might have laughed over the obviously rhetorical question.

"You're stronger when you combine your magic with his. I tested you three times. And three times you worked together. First with the flood, then with the mountain lion, and then with the fire. Catriona and Deirdre have failed to open a portal." Hamish released a loud sigh of disappointment. "So you, dear Eliza, will channel yourself through him. If you don't, I'll dispose of your sisters once and for all."

Frightened by the threat, Eliza sought to make a plan.

Did she really need Boggs's help? She'd opened doorways before. But the bubble she had created to protect her and Kit from the fire had been something new, as if she had bent the doorway back on itself. She had never accomplished such a complicated manipulation of time and space. Was it possible that Kit's presence had enhanced her abilities?

If true, what other extraordinary things could she accomplish with him by her side?

"I'll need a platter, a wand, a chalice, a dagger, a sword, and a whip," she said, trying to stall.

Hamish laughed as if she'd told an amusing joke. "No."

"Then I can't possibly perform the ritual of summoning."

"I'm not giving you a sword *and* a whip. I've read the grimoire."

"Then you know the tools are necessary."

He eyed her. "Perhaps. However, a good witch doesn't need tools."

"Maybe I'm not a good witch," she replied coolly.

"Don't try my patience." He handed her a smooth piece of dark wood about two feet long. "Will this do?"

As soon as she touched the wand, her hand warmed from the energy present. Using a device not her own was folly.

She flicked it from her bound hands in an act of desecration. "You know I can't use that."

"Then why are we still talking? It is November Eve, and this place is touched by the Hallow."

They stood in sacred space? Eliza glanced around the cave. Hallows harbored both the seen and the unseen, and were places where the dead could cross into the material plane. But The Horseman wasn't dead. He was a spirit beyond that. She wasn't certain why the Hallow would be necessary to Hamish's plan, but the in-between place—where the realms of the manifest and the non-manifest could co-exist—would increase the likelihood of successful contact with the other side.

"If we stand in a Hallow, then why don't you contact him yourself?" she asked.

"Believe me," Hamish said through gritted teeth, "I've tried. Enough talk. Do it. Now."

She stepped to the stone altar. Hamish cocked his head to his men, and they shoved Kit to one side. Hamish stood in the north position, she in the south, and Kit to the west.

"I need my hands free," she said. "I need ash. And it would be helpful to have someone in the east."

Hamish waved at one of his men, who went to the iron cage and pulled Dee out. While she was dragged to the open side of the altar, Hamish cut Eliza's hands free.

Eliza rubbed her wrists as she saw fear in Dee's eyes. Her cousin—no, her sister, if Hamish was to be believed—flicked her gaze from Kerr to Boggs. Eliza slid a glance at Kit, wondering if he was still alive, so quiet had his energy been during all of this.

She focused on the task at hand. Normally, she would prepare herself for a summoning by bathing in saltwater and consuming water purified in sunlight, but since that ritual wasn't possible she tried to quiet her mind, no easy task considering the circumstances.

One of Hamish's men scooped ash from the remnants of a nearby campfire, then dumped it onto the altar. Eliza smoothed out the pile with the palm of her hand. Using her forefinger, she traced out a triangle. Inside, she added the symbol for The Horseman—a bow and arrow. Then she placed her left hand, palm down, atop the symbol and whispered the incantation under her breath.

"The protector of the unseen, and the shadows that beckon;
The giver of visions, and the keeper of ancient words.

146

I call you, Horseman, to pass through the veils.
I call you, Horace, to leave the darkness and walk in the path
of light."

Eliza opened her eyes. The shock on Hamish's face tugged a faint smile to her lips.

He sputtered in a hushed tone. "How do you know his name?"

The one thing needed to summon the spirit that had watched over the McCulloch women for hundreds of years had never been inscribed into the grimoire. Eliza knew, even as a young child, that this had been a special—and secret—gift given to her. She hoped she hadn't just made a terrible mistake.

"He told me," she said.

CHAPTER EIGHT

K it knew immediately when The Horseman entered the vicinity. The whispers began once again in his ears. He had suspected that Hamish had somehow suppressed them, and now it would seem this Horseman had the ability to overcome Hamish's influence.

A wind blew through the cavern, lifting Eliza's hair into a web-like dance. It was obvious Eliza was stronger than her sisters, and not because the other two women had been chained and imprisoned. Something in Eliza pulsed loud and clear. She was a channel. This place that served as a Hallow for Hamish was enhanced by Eliza's presence. It was apparent now that Kit needed her to accomplish his task. And Hamish obviously needed her, as well.

The Horseman controls one of the entryways to the other side, his granny began chatting in his ear. *Your McCulloch witch is more powerful than I'd thought. Why are you still with her?*

Kit didn't respond, since the answer was more involved than he cared to admit.

A dust devil of spinning dirt formed and grew larger just beyond them. When the melee settled, a giant man with a muscled torso stood before them. A large bow was secured to his back and a beard of shrubs and leaves spilled from his face. As his gaze took in those before him, his countenance seemed to slump ever so slightly, a look of resignation settling over him.

"Hamish," he said. "This is forbidden."

Hamish stepped closer to the spirit that Eliza had summoned. "You won't speak to me. It's been eons. It's been long enough."

The Horseman shifted his focus to Eliza. "Why have you done this?"

"He gave me no choice. He threatened Catriona and Deirdre. Who is he? What has he done to warrant your disfavor?"

Hamish began to pace. "It was all a misunderstanding. Let me come home."

The Horseman locked his gaze onto Kit but said nothing. Instead, he answered Eliza's question. "Hamish is my son. There was a time when he was lazy and careless, and allowed much to cross the barrier from here to there and there to here."

"I said I was sorry," Hamish cried.

The Horseman ignored him. "So his access was denied."

"You abandoned me here. I want to come home!"

"But you have not behaved while living amongst the humans, have you?"

Hamish scoffed. "You expect too much. Was I not allowed to play with them? It's been an eternity. What else was I to do?"

"I had hoped the time away would strengthen your convictions, but instead, you practice the dark arts."

"You left me with humans. They're gutless, immoral, and without honor."

"So you sink to their level?" The Horseman demanded.

Hamish trembled. "I did what I had to in order to survive."

"Perhaps." The Horseman looked at the men with Hamish. "Unchain the McCulloch girl." He indicated Cat, who was still restrained in her iron cage. The men obeyed. Eliza rushed over and helped Cat from the prison and to her feet. Dee joined them.

"Is it true that Hamish is our father?" Eliza's voice echoed off the cavern walls.

"Hamish believes himself to have beget all three of you—I believe in an effort to gain access to a Hallow such as this one—but he isn't your father, Eliza."

"Then who is?" she asked.

But Kit knew. And from Eliza's expression, she suspected as well.

"But how?" She looked at The Horseman, at her father. "You're not … human."

"I was dismayed when I saw that Hamish was seducing females to produce children with enhanced gifts. Your mother and her sisters weren't the first women with whom he succeeded, but they were by far the most powerful. The McCulloch line is steeped in enchantment. But I managed to get to Marta in time, to undo the spell of the child in her womb. But to save the life that had already begun to grow, I had to weave myself into the seed. I gave you the breath of life, the breath of *my* life."

"That's why you told me your name," she said quietly.

"And it's why we've always been able to connect so easily. You are my beloved daughter, Eliza McCulloch."

"And I'm your son!" Hamish yelled. "Where is the love and mercy for me? I'm sick and tired of living in this place. Please, by all things holy, let me come home."

An eerie stillness settled. The air became chilled, and a tingle ran down Kit's spine.

It was here.

Just as he'd hoped, *El Viejo del Saco* had followed Hamish.

And Kit was ready for him.

CHAPTER NINE

E liza couldn't breathe.

With panic in her eyes, Dee grabbed hold of Eliza's hand, but Eliza couldn't hear what she was saying. The world began to close in as Dee tried to keep her from falling to the ground. She struggled to speak, but Dee didn't seem to understand.

What was happening?

Strong arms bolstered her from behind as Eliza felt herself slipping away. Black wings spanned out and encircled her.

She gasped, able to inhale air again. She was in the cave, with everyone also present, but their forms were muted and distant.

"We don't have much time." Kit's voice echoed around her.

She spun around.

They were in the cave, but out of phase. He must have shifted to his crow form and shielded her, and then she had brought them both to this parallel place inside the Hallow.

Kit filled the space, half-man and half-crow, a blending that continuously shifted before her. He spread his wings wide, the feathers as black as a starless night sky. Around him, within him, a void was forming, a swirling vortex that tugged at her. She shifted her stance to avoid being sucked in.

"What are you?" Her voice trembled.

"I'm a fighter, Eliza, for the balance of good and evil. There's a creature attached to Hamish called *El Viejo del Saco*, and I'm here to destroy it."

"What can I do?"

"He was trying to take hold of you. I managed to stop him, and you brought us here. When I capture him, can you send him from the earthly plane in the same way?"

"I ... I don't know."

"Is it true that your skills have increased since being near me?"

"Yes."

"Then *use* me, Eliza."

"How?"

"Since I've met you, my skills have changed, as well. I've never fully been The Crow, and as far as I know, neither have my brothers possessed the skills I seem to be acquiring. I can only guess it's because of you. If I can capture the demon, I'll need a prison. One that can be sealed for all time. Can you access a dimension not of this time or place? Can you open it so that I can banish *El Viejo del Saco* once and for all?"

With panic clawing in her belly, she nodded, the gesture stiff and disjointed.

"Eliza, you can't leave the portal open once I enter. You need to close it as soon as possible. Do you understand?"

Her heart began to break, sliding into despair in the same way the flood had knocked her from her feet and carried her away.

No!

An energy—fierce and strong and white-hot—burst inside her.

Now that I've found you, Boggs, I'm not letting you go.

She squared her shoulders. She wasn't going to lose him without a fight, to hell with the dictum that a Boggs and a McCulloch should never join forces, should never share their bodies, should never fall in love.

If she was enhanced by Kit's presence, then it stood to reason that Dee and Cat would be, as well. Her cousins were strong witches in their own right, and although Hamish had beaten them down and somehow dampened their abilities, if Eliza could revive them then they could help. There was power in three. And three McCulloch witches boosted with the presence of The Crow might have the capability to prevail in a way that none of them ever could alone.

CHAPTER TEN

When Kit shifted back from the bubble Eliza had created, it was clear that one way or another he would banish the demon parasite that Hamish had likely enabled for centuries. If he didn't, then not only was the world at risk, but even more pressing, so was Eliza.

As soon as *El Viejo del Saco* appeared, it had immediately gone for Eliza. Why not her cousins, Cat and Dee, weakened from a lengthy captivity at the hands of Hamish? It had to be Eliza's energy. It wanted her. Kit had to make it want him.

An old man carrying a sack now stood near Hamish, and he didn't take his eyes from Eliza. *El Viejo del Saco* had taken form. It was said The Bag Man drank the blood of misbehaving children, but Kit didn't doubt that he would go for an adult if that was his only option. And he'd chosen his target.

"You've got baggage attached, Hamish," The Horseman said. "I warned you."

"What?" Hamish cried. "Him?" He glanced at the hunched man standing nearby.

Kit stepped carefully, moving slowly to reach Hamish and the creature.

"He won't come with me," Hamish continued in a rush, then said to the old man, "*El Sacomán*, I have no children for you. The Crow promised them, but it seems he was lying."

The Bag Man's eyes glittered as he stared at Eliza. "I will have her, instead." His brittle voice grated like metal on metal.

Like hell.

Kit spied a knife on the belt of one of Hamish's men. With the man's attention riveted to the family spat between Hamish and his father, Kit reached over and yanked the small blade free. He slashed his left palm then held the weapon at arm's length as the man he'd taken it from tried to attack.

"Stand back," Kit warned.

Ignoring the pain from the self-inflicted wound, he squeezed his hand tight, the blood dripping in rivulets to the dirt floor. The Bag Man sniffed and turned toward him. Pulling Dee with her, Eliza scrambled toward Cat, and the three of them crouched together.

Hamish frowned as Kit moved closer, then his expression turned to one of dawning realization. He burst out laughing. "You're strong, Crow, but you can't kill *El Sacomán*."

"I'm not here to kill him."

Open the portal, Eliza.

The old man dropped his dark knapsack and approached Kit, lured by the smell of blood. Kit let his crow form take over, spreading his wings and flapping. He snatched *El Viejo del Saco* with his talons and ascended to the cavern's ceiling, searching for some sign that Eliza had opened a doorway for him.

The Bag Man squirmed and shifted, and then he bit Kit's soft flesh just above the talon. Shocked that the old man even had teeth, Kit squawked and lost his grip on the demon, dropping him to the floor. As he swooped down to grab him again, Eliza bolted forward and wrapped her arms around the creature. And then, they were gone.

"BRING HER BACK," KIT DEMANDED.

"I don't interfere in the world of humans," The Horseman replied.

"Bullshit. You meddle with the McCullochs all the time."

"That is guidance."

"Eliza's your daughter! You said so yourself. And now you would abandon her to an eternity locked with *El Viejo del Saco*?"

"She chose her path."

"It was supposed to be me, not her." Kit's voice cracked. "She broke our agreement."

"On the contrary. It would seem she sacrificed herself for you."

Why? Why would she do this?

Kit turned to Dee, sitting with an arm around Catriona. "Can either of you find her? You obviously helped her to do this."

Dee shook her head. "We barely aided her. She simply used us to create a triumvirate. She's always been the strongest McCulloch."

"It is time for me to go," The Horseman said.

Anger filled Kit, and he swelled in size, flapping his wings wide and screeching in frustration.

Hamish skirted around Kit, flinching. "Please let me come with you," he pleaded to his father.

With a look of resignation, The Horseman nodded. "The least I can do is remove you from this world and stop you from causing any more harm. But there will be consequences, son." He allowed Hamish to enter the portal. It closed, leaving a heavy, thick silence in its wake.

The cave was now just a cave—dank with the strong scent of the earth filling the air.

Kit returned to human form and sank to the ground.

"Granny?" He would plead like Hamish if it brought Eliza back.

There's no trace of her, Kester, and you'd do well to put her out of your mind and move on.

"There must be something you can do. Something *I* can do. Tell me."

I cannot condone this.

"Why?" His voice filled the cave, startling Dee and Cat. He needed to take them out of here, but he had to be certain there wasn't a way to find Eliza. He had no intention of leaving if she could still be found.

You never did pay attention as a boy, so listen now. Eliza's grandfather was Iain McCulloch. Her grandmother, Beitiris, was Iain's third wife. Both of his previous wives died, as well as their babes.

"What does this have to do with me?"

Iain's first wife was my sister, Elspeth. She perished in childbirth. Iain was cursed, and he's contaminated his offspring. I won't let another Boggs suffer for it.

"But the fact that Eliza lives proves your theory wrong."

No. It just proves that Beitiris was smarter than I gave her credit. She was but eighteen years old when she wed Iain in his old age, but she must have known her fate was sealed. She must have known the rumors that swirled around him. And she worked dark magic to protect herself, her daughters, and their daughters.

A dawning realization hit Kit. "The grimoire," he murmured.

A book of Beitiris's secrets.

"Exactly."

Maybe it held the key to finding Eliza.

He stood and explored around the altar until he found a bag. A search produced the tome that Hamish had stolen. Kit set it on the altar and began flipping through the pages, but he couldn't make sense of it.

Dee moved beside him, and he showed her the open book.

"It's in Gaelic," she said.

"Can you read it?"

Dee spent a long moment scanning several pages. "I'm sorry but this is beyond me."

"What about you?" he asked Catriona.

She shook her head. "But Marta could."

"Eliza's mother," Dee clarified. "We should return the book to her and our mothers anyway."

Kit hesitated, not wanting to leave.

"She's not here." Dee's quiet voice was filled with compassion.

His throat threatened to close. "Then I'll take you both home."

Dee's gaze faltered. "I'll be honest with you. You won't be welcome."

Kit remained silent, prompting Dee to explain herself.

"Our grandfather's first wife was a Boggs. It was said that she practiced dark arts to ensnare him."

"But she died in childbirth."

"Our granny, who was our grandfather's third wife, believed that your ancestor's spells backfired. We were always told to stay away from your family. You're all no good." But the slight smile on her face took the sting from her words.

"Do you believe that?"

"After what's happened? No."

Cat moved beside Dee. "I'm with Dee. We'd be much obliged for your help in getting us home. And we'll put in a good word with our mothers. We'll try to help you find Eliza."

Kit nodded, setting his mind on the future. Somehow, some way, he'd find Eliza McCulloch. And he'd convince her there was no such thing as a Boggs curse—or a McCulloch one, for that matter. Each side blamed the other. It was time to put an end to it.

With one final glance around the cave, he took one of the torches and led Eliza's sisters to freedom.

CHAPTER ELEVEN

Taos, New Mexico Territory
November

K it sat across from Marta McCulloch, the kitchen table sanded to a shiny smoothness. Everything in the home—a multi-room adobe dwelling on the outskirts of town—spoke of an attention to style and refinement.

Eliza's resemblance to her mother was strong, with the same oval-shaped face and lips pressed into a worried frown, reminding Kit of the first time he had seen Eliza on the main street of La Noria. The familiar ache pulsed, and he tensed, waiting for it to pass. He *would* see her again.

The McCulloch Grimoire sat on the table before Marta, and she watched Kit with haunted eyes. This was where she and her daughter differed—Eliza's gaze had flashed with urgency and determination, with fire, but Marta's brown eyes reflected sadness along with a palpable disdain. For him.

"I want to find her," he said. "You need to set aside this Boggs and McCulloch feud."

"My daughter is gone *because* of you." Marta's voice rose, and she swallowed hard as she paused to take a shaky breath. "So how dare you tell me that McCullochs don't suffer at the hands of a Boggs."

He didn't have time to change her mind. The truth she spoke sent a sharp pain through his gut, but he didn't have time for that either.

"Will you help me?" he pressed. "All that matters right now is getting her back."

She glanced down at the book, twisting her lips into a scowl. "I dreamed of possessing the grimoire again, but not at this price."

"Can you read it? Can you possibly find *anything* in it that might help us?"

She raised her gaze, suspicion haunting her eyes. "I'll look. Come back this evening."

Kit would take any bit of hope he could. "Thank you."

KIT SAT ON A WOODEN BENCH CARVED WITH BIRDS, CERTAIN THEY WERE crows. Marta faced him on a stuffed sofa with Dee and Cat beside her. Behind them stood Aileen and Rose, watching him with impassive expressions.

They were a formidable bunch.

Clasping the grimoire on her lap, Marta gave a shake of her head and twisted her mouth in frustration. "I still can't believe a goddamned Boggs is in my house."

"Aunt Marta," Dee admonished.

"Did you find anything?" Kit couldn't mask his impatience.

"Maybe." She expelled a deep breath. "It's been nineteen years since we last had this book. We did our best to recreate it from memory, but it seems we may have misinterpreted some of it."

"And?" Kit asked.

"Let me ask you first: How long have you been The Crow?"

"It started when I was a boy."

"And you are Bonnie Boggs's grandson." The accusation dripped from her lips.

"Yes, ma'am."

"Eliza has always had the gift of the liminal, the in-between space. It's a place that's not a place, and a time that's not a time. Dee and Cat told me what happened in the cave, and the truth of Eliza's father." She paused. "That would explain her heightened abilities."

Kit thought she was taking it well, producing a child with a man who wasn't human.

"I have the gift of augury," she continued.

Kit gave her a questioning look.

"It's divination using birds. And you are thick with crow energy." He didn't want to be rude, but they were wasting time.

Always so impatient, Kester.

Granny? She'd been so adamant about not wanting to help him rescue a McCulloch.

I'm here because I'm curious. And because you're my grandson, and I love you. I can't let you face this cackle of witches alone.

"There's an entire chapter in the grimoire on crows," Marta said. "It quite surprised us. Granny Bea wrote it after a vision from a seer."

"What does it say?" Kit asked.

"It speaks of the triformis—one entity with three aspects. I understand there are three of you?"

Kit nodded. If he needed Jack and Callum present to find Eliza then he would fetch them, but the delay would be costly. Not the least of which would be to his sanity. "What else?" he pressed.

She narrowed her eyes. "It seems rather prophetic, actually. To enter the place that is betwixt and between, a triformis of crows is needed, along with the bones."

"Bones of what?"

"That which you seek."

Kit frowned. "Do you have a bone from Eliza?"

"Of course not. But thanks to Catriona, we have the Bag Man's finger."

"We do?"

"When you grabbed him in the cave, your claw must have severed it," Cat said.

"She kept her wits and retrieved it," Marta said, approval in her tone. "We're lucky she did. But it seems we're even more lucky to have a crow with us."

"It will take too long to gather my brothers," Kit said.

"I agree. I think you will be enough. Dee and Cat will complete the trinity."

"What do we do?"

"The moon will rise after midnight. We'll perform the ritual then."

"What do you need from me?" he asked.

Marta smiled grimly. "We need you to summon a murder of crows."

CHAPTER TWELVE

U ntil the incident with Eliza and the flash flood, Kit had never
called forth a flock of crows. In truth, it had never occurred to
him to do such a thing. It would seem there were skills he possessed
that he was still discovering.

He followed the McCulloch women to a place in the nearby Taos
hills. Marta led them, a torch in her hand, but Kit needed no light. He
was comfortable in the shadows.

I can hear the tone of your accusation, Granny said into his ear.

"You never told me I could summon crows." He spoke aloud, in a
low voice.

*Even in the afterlife, there are limits to what I can see. And there's that
damned Comanche blood in you. Combined with your Scottish ancestry, it's
been fascinating to watch.*

"Maybe it has more to do with my proximity to a McCulloch."

Hogwash! Don't try to justify your lust for that girl.

When he didn't immediately respond, his granny released a grunt
of dissatisfaction. *Oh, no. You are not falling in love with that witch.*

"It's not up to you. And why don't you hover over Jack and Cal
this much?"

They're not trying to romance a McCulloch! Besides, they can't hear me.

The terrain became steeper, so Kit stopped the conversation. At last, he crested the top of a mesa, a flat expanse of red rock greeting them, and tried to catch his breath. Marta set to work laying out a large pentagram on the ground in gray ash from a bag she had brought with her, while Aileen held the light.

Once the star was complete, Rose unwrapped the remains of the Bag Man's finger and placed it at the center of the star, then carefully stepped back and lifted her skirt to avoid dislodging the lines of ash.

Marta motioned him over. "If you'll stand at the center, Kester Boggs, Cat and Dee will be on either side of you. Rose, Aileen, and I will watch the remaining points of the pentagram to offer our support."

Kit silently agreed, still unsure how to go about this. He wanted to ask Marta, but he sensed that she wasn't certain about the exact parts of the ritual, either. He moved to the center of the star, reminding him of the protective bubble Eliza had created around the two of them. It had completely kept the raging fire away from them. How could he open a doorway? That was Eliza's skill, not his, and from the way Marta told it, none of the other McCulloch women could do it, either.

Quit overthinking it, Kester.

As the women surrounded him at each of their posts, he thought about when he was a boy. He'd always used his gifts by feel, by gut instinct. Perhaps he needed to trust himself. Perhaps he needed to let his heart guide him. It was a novel idea. He'd never chased a woman to the other side. He'd never chased a woman, period.

The McCulloch women began to murmur, quietly chanting an incantation. He breathed deeply and closed his eyes. Immediately, he felt the flurry of crows flying in the distance. A simple shift brought him into the flock—*the murder*—of the swarm. Pumping his wings, he flowed across the sky, eyeing the terrain as it glowed in an otherworldly, grayish hue. He was man, but he was also crow, and from his vantage point, he could see the illumination emanating from the pentagram on the ground far below. It exuded upward, beckoning the murder toward it.

As the birds neared, Kit experienced the sensation of being sucked into a narrow tunnel, spiraling downward. Still in crow form, he landed with a thump in a small, dark cave. The Bag Man and Eliza both sat across from him, arms resting on their knees and their heads hanging low, a picture of utter defeat.

Kit cawed, and Eliza snapped her head up, shock registering in her eyes when she saw him.

"Boggs?" she whispered.

But Kit couldn't revert to human form.

As Eliza bolted to her feet so did the Bag Man, casting a wary eye at Kit. Eliza tried to step forward, but *El Viejo del Saco* grabbed her arm and held her in place. It was surprising the old man had enough strength, but he successfully held her back.

Eliza suddenly split into two. The Bag Man released her, clearly confused.

Kit swiveled his avian head to see better.

There were two Elizas.

Certain he knew which one was real, Kit nudged her with his beak. The other Eliza shook her head.

The Bag Man tried to grab hold of Kit's wing. Kit batted him away, but the old man was tenacious. Kit flapped his wings and hopped around, squawking and trying to shake the demon. If he couldn't determine which Eliza was real, then he'd take them both.

The women scrambled to climb onto his back, but The Bag Man wouldn't stop his clambering. With a surge, Kit took flight but stopped short of climbing higher, both because he had three passengers and because he didn't want to hit the ceiling of this place, if that was even possible. He had no idea.

One of the Elizas jumped and yanked *El Viejo del Saco* free, both falling downward.

In horror, Kit was about to drop back to the ground when the doorway opened, and he was thrust from the cave. He fell in a heap to the center of the pentagram with Eliza atop him.

He sat up, clutching her to him.

Was it her?

It's her.

"How do you know?" he asked his grandmother.

In my physical life, I could see fetches—doubles. In this life, I can make *doubles.*

Kit folded Eliza into his arms, burying his face into her hair. "Thank you."

Eliza leaned back to look at him. "For what?" She misunderstood him, thinking he was speaking to her.

Instead of answering, he kissed her.

Someone cleared their throat, reminding him they were surrounded by Eliza's mother, aunts, and cousins. He came to his feet and helped Eliza to stand. Marta hugged her daughter fiercely, and Kit was forced to step back as the other women took their turn at the heartfelt reunion.

I forbid this union. The voice wasn't Granny.

Beitiris McCulloch, it's about time you showed up, Granny Boggs answered. *And for all things sacred, I forbid the union as well.*

"It's not up to either of you," Kit said.

The living McCulloch women all turned to look at him.

"You certainly talk to yourself too much," Marta said. "I can't imagine what Eliza sees in you."

"Mother," Eliza admonished and turned to Kit. "I can't believe you came for me."

"There was no way I wouldn't." He didn't bother to hide the hunger in his eyes.

A smile slowly stretched across Eliza's lips, widening into a full-blown grin as she watched him.

If mated to a Boggs, Eliza will die and any children she has will die, Beitiris said.

Hogwash, Granny Boggs replied. *If Kit is bound to a McCulloch, then he will die.*

"Enough!" Kit roared, causing Eliza and the others to jump. He quickly added, "Not you. I've got two bickering women in my ear who won't shut up."

He went on to explain his ability to hear spirits and reiterated everything the two old women had told him. It wasn't that he believed in this curse business, but he wanted Eliza to make up her own mind.

"If you fear the outcome of us together," Kit said to her, "then I'll respect your wishes. But I want you, Eliza." He waited and looked into her eyes. Her presence warmed him through like sunshine after a stormy day. "Curses only work if you believe them. And I don't."

Eliza took hold of his hand. "I will walk beside you, Crow, in this life and the next."

And with that, Kit sealed his fate and healed the past.

Granny Boggs sighed into his ear. *I expect the first female child to be named Bonnie.*

Granny Bea chimed in. *No! I insist on Beitiris.*

Kit nuzzled the side of Eliza's cheek. "Can you create a doorway where our grandmothers can't follow?"

Eliza grinned and nodded. "With you by my side, I can."

CHAPTER THIRTEEN

F lush with nervous excitement, Eliza grabbed hold of Kit's hand and led him to the small adobe shack on the McCulloch property that served as an apothecary, which brought her mother and aunts a modest income. It was the only place where Eliza could hope for privacy.

During the past two weeks, Kit had stayed in town and Eliza had been careful to avoid time alone with him in his rented room, not wanting to instigate any rumors. This was mostly out of respect for her mother. Although many townsfolk came to the McCullochs for remedies to minor ailments, there were still some who viewed the six women as tainted, and therefore to be feared and avoided. Eliza had no desire to add 'women of ill-repute' to the list.

Finally, however, she couldn't deny the need to have private time with Boggs. They'd passed their days developing a tentative friendship, because while Eliza felt her connection to Kit clear down to her bones, would it be enough for a lifetime? It had seemed prudent to spend time getting to know one another, although it had proved a challenge to keep the simmering attraction between them under control considering the way Boggs looked at her whenever they were together.

It was finally time to do something about it.

"You're not leading me to some witch's ritual, are you?" Kit asked as she tugged him into the dwelling.

"Why would you say that?" She released his hand and shut the door, then fumbled for a match and lit a candle on the side table.

"The moon is full, and the time is close to midnight." The flickering light cast his features into dancing shadows, his dark eyes intent on her.

She shivered, anticipating what it would be like to be fully joined with him. "You're so suspicious."

"It's in my nature, Eliza." A wicked gleam flashed in his gaze. "I'm beginning to think you want to be alone with me, but are you certain?"

A tenuous smile reached her lips. "So certain I brought bedding."

He raised an eyebrow, then his expression became solemn. "You don't have to do this," he replied, his words soft, quiet. "I'm not going anywhere. You've already bewitched me. I can wait."

"For what?" she asked, her voice breathless.

He considered her for a moment before replying. "For you not to flee when I ask for your hand."

Her heart pounded. "What makes you think I would flee?"

"I think you're not quite certain about me."

She remained silent, for there was some truth in it. The pull he exerted over her mind and her senses—and her body—was overwhelming. He was always in her thoughts, from sunup to sundown. But what of his crow nature?

"I've never known a man like you," she admitted, releasing the burden that had been weighing on her.

"I'm just a man, Eliza. You hold far more cards in the strange department than I do."

"How so?"

"As the daughter of The Horseman, I can only imagine that you're immortal. As I age, you'll remain as young and beautiful as ever."

"I never thought of that," she murmured. "Do you think I might live forever?"

He cupped her face with his right hand and caressed her cheek with his thumb. "We might only have fifty or sixty years before I'm too old to keep up with you, so if you're ready to start our life together then I'm more than game."

He drew her close and kissed her. His lips were warm, and yet Eliza shivered. She'd never been with a man, and she'd never thought she would marry, but if the fates were allowing her to have both, she wasn't about to let Kester Boggs go, despite the dark cloud that hovered over the connection between their families. But she had a thought about that, as well.

His arms encircled her, and she sank into his embrace as the kiss deepened. They had done as much these past few weeks, and like those times, her body came to life with a craving for more. But while they had always stopped, this time she had every intention of showing Kit that she wanted to be with him…completely.

Cat and Dee had told her how distraught he'd been when she had disappeared with The Bag Man. What a vile creature *El Viejo del Saco* had been. During her time in the prison she'd managed to create, she had been exhausted fighting him off as he sought to drain her energy and she'd been unable to leave. The demon spirit had remained too close to her. Had she opened a doorway, he would have simply escaped. After a good long while, she'd begun to give up hope of ever returning to this time and this plane, where those she loved resided.

But Kit hadn't given up. And he'd found a way to her.

She wrapped her arms around his neck and gave herself fully to exploring his mouth with hers, her senses heightened with arousal. She reveled in his masculine smell, the stubble on his cheeks, the thick tresses of his hair. Her hands roamed along his shoulders and down to the corded muscles of his arms, and she tugged at the hem of his shirt until she touched bare skin. He assisted by pulling the garb over his head.

As she continued to investigate the hard planes of his chest with her hands and lips, he brought a palm to her breast and gently kneaded. She leaned into him, letting him know that he was free to continue. He released the buttons on her blouse then leaned down and kissed the top of her breasts. As he went lower, she raked her fingers through his hair, and then shrugged her arms free of the garment. He inched her chemise up until he could push it over her head. With his access to her no longer impeded by clothing, he began plundering her in earnest with his lips.

She gasped, finding it difficult to stand. His hands caught her at the waist and he stood, gathering her against him. They were finally skin to skin, with the evidence of his arousal obvious. Trepidation filled her, immediately giving way to a fierce need. She didn't want to stop. From the first moment she had locked gazes with The Crow, in that room crowded with the other women Hamish had abducted, a jolt of awareness had sliced through her. Come what may, she was his. She would give him her body on this night, with the iridescent light of the full moon glowing through the window, and she suspected that her soul would soon follow.

As she stepped back, he resisted the parting by tugging her close again.

"Let me get the blankets," she whispered. "And then I will finally pleasure you."

A low and throaty laugh escaped him, but he let her cross the room to retrieve the bedding. She spread it onto the wood floor, unlaced her boots and kicked them aside, then wriggled free of her skirt. Once she was completely naked, she turned to him. He had been watching, and now moved slowly toward her.

"You're beautiful, Eliza." He caressed her lightly with a fingertip from her collarbone to the roundness of her breast and then along the curve of her hip.

The reverence in the action, accompanied by the hungry look in his eyes, made her feel powerful and desired.

She tugged at the waistband of his trousers. "Just don't change into crow form, please. My mother is already convinced that if we have children, they might be …"

He had stilled, so she glanced up. Then, he laughed.

Eliza bit her lip, unsure whether to join him.

"As I said before, I'm just a man. This coupling is far more dangerous for me."

Eliza released an exasperated sigh. "And I'm just a woman, despite whatever … blood may run through me. Speaking of which, can we go to Scotland? Soon?"

He lowered his gaze to her uncovered flesh. "Eliza, I will give you whatever you want."

Her body heated, and she didn't want to wait any longer. "What I want is you."

He shed the remainder of his clothing and guided her to the blankets, bracing his body over hers. With his mouth, he fawned over her breasts with much greater urgency, and soon her hips were lifting, beckoning him, but he continued to torment her.

"Crow, please."

He brought his face to hers. "It's my job to bring *you* pleasure."

"You have," she groaned. "Now get on with it." Raising her head, her mouth crushed against his, and she tugged at his lips with her teeth.

He slid his free hand beneath her buttocks and entered her in one swift thrust. Her breath caught as he filled her. Soon the pain eased, and her body began to move with a need and rhythm all its own. Wrapping her legs around him, she held him tightly, quickly reaching a precipice, and he whispered her name as she careened down the other side, flying across the land. As one with The Crow, she was stripped of earthly constraints and soared toward the stars.

The desperate need she'd felt just moments ago dissipated, and in its wake came a happy bliss.

Kit raised his head and gently kissed her. "And now, Eliza McCulloch, will you marry me?"

She smiled and held him close. "On one condition."

"Anything."

"Will you write a grimoire? The Crow Grimoire? It would be for our children."

"I'm not much of a writer."

She ran her hands down the length of his back. "I can help you. I don't want to lose the knowledge that you and your brothers possess."

He kissed her again, and she felt him stir inside of her.

"We can do this again?" she asked, surprised.

"Yes. Unless you're sore."

She was, a little. But she was certain that it would pass. "No. And yes."

He gave her a questioning look. "No, I'm not sore, and yes, I'll marry you."

"Then I'll love you one more time." His breath tickled her neck.

"And I'll love you right back, Crow."

CHAPTER FOURTEEN

Scotland
Six months later

K it stood beside Eliza at Iain McCulloch's grave, a large headstone marking the site. Dark clouds threatened with rain, and Kit could have done without the constant wind, but otherwise he was happy to accompany his wife on her first visit to the homeland.

"Ready?" she asked, bright green eyes watching him.

"Whatever you say, Witch."

He planned to spend a lifetime soaking up that gaze.

Amusement danced in her eyes.

She held out her hand and he placed his much larger one on it, palm up. She produced a small knife from a pocket in her gray wool coat and slashed a shallow cut across his callused flesh. She folded his fingers over it, then did the same wound to herself. They both held their fists over the grave, squeezing as first one, then two, then three drops of blood were released.

Eliza spoke,

> *"Blood to blood,*
> *we are one.*

Under the moon,
and under the sun.
Heal the land and heal the past,
for the crow shall inherit the earth at last."

The birds descended from the sky, a wave of black undulating on the air currents, releasing a torrent of loud caws.

Kit pulled a cotton cloth from his coat and wrapped it around Eliza's hand to stop the bleeding. She smiled at him. "Now we can be sure."

"I was always sure." He took her other hand and led her down the gently sloping hillside. "And now I would like to bed my wife."

A husky laugh escaped Eliza. "You're telling me that you never once worried about the McCulloch curse?"

"Have you worried over the Boggs black magic?"

"No."

"But I'm glad that you did what you thought you should, for both our families. It's time I planted a babe in you."

Eliza walked quickly to keep pace with him. "Are you saying that you've held back all these months?" she asked, out of breath.

He stopped and faced her, unable to hide his annoyance. "It would seem our grandmothers have somehow prevented a child."

"What? How? You've been so ... thorough." Her cheeks blushed a deep red.

Kit grinned. "I'm glad you noticed." He stole a quick kiss. "Granny Boggs informed me this morning, saying it was for our own good. But she added that once we completed the ritual at Iain's grave, she and Bea would allow it. She's even agreed that our daughter shall be named Beitiris, since Jack and Hannah called their daughter Bonnie."

"Well, how gracious of your granny. And mine." But the tinge of disdain in her voice wasn't hard to miss.

Kit pulled her into his arms. "I have an idea," he said, his lips hovering near hers. "Open a doorway, and I'll take you someplace no one will find us, in either this world or the next."

"It's a deal."

She captured his mouth, and it soon became too heated to continue out in the open. They returned to the Inn—located on the edge of the town of Inverness—where they had moved the day before. Too much spirit activity at Culloden Moor had made their previous lodging difficult for Kit, and Eliza had been unable to help either him or the ghosts, the location still haunted by the violent battle of 1746.

Once in the privacy of their room, Kit set to work undressing his wife, revealing first her bared feet, then shapely legs and arms, and finally her full breasts. He suckled and nipped and teased her with his mouth until she was writhing with need.

Had she opened a path to an in-between place? He didn't want to stop and ask, his own desire reaching a boiling point. He thrust hard and deep into her, and she accepted him fully, matching him with equal intensity. It had been like this since that night on the McCulloch homestead. It still startled him how easy this was with her. She fit him perfectly, and she was everything he wasn't. In Eliza he saw the sweet beauty of the flowers, the comforting ebb and flow of the tide, the wink of Father Sun and the magic of Mother Moon. She was the whisper of all good things. He'd fought evil for so long that he had forgotten there was another way to live. Eliza had opened that door for him.

The need to produce a child with her pressed on him with an untenable urgency, and he savored her luscious release as he spilled his seed into her. As his hunger abated and his body relaxed, he remained with her. He knew he would want her again soon.

He shifted so as not to crush her, but his body still blanketed hers. Biting her neck, he felt the breath of her sigh against his cheek, and she raked her fingers down his back. He raised himself on an elbow to behold the face of his ravished wife, and that's when he noticed the area around the bed.

"Where are we?" he asked.

"Hmmm."

"Eliza."

She cracked open one eye and whispered, "You told me to open a doorway."

It wasn't so much what Kit could see as what he felt. They were still in their room at the Inn, but Kit knew that weren't in the same time.

"When are we?"

"We are before the McCulloch-Boggs feud, before the darkness that descended on Iain McCulloch. We have created life without the burden of all that came before."

The intelligence of his wife never ceased to amaze him. "This child will have a clean slate."

"Something like that."

"I love you, Witch."

She snuggled closer. "And I love you, Crow."

WOULD YOU CONSIDER POSTING A REVIEW OF *THE CROW BROTHERS Collection*? Not only does it help other readers discover a book, it also aids an author in pursuing promotional opportunities. My heartfelt thanks. ~ Kristy

If you enjoy western romances with a paranormal twist, don't miss
Into The Land Of Shadows

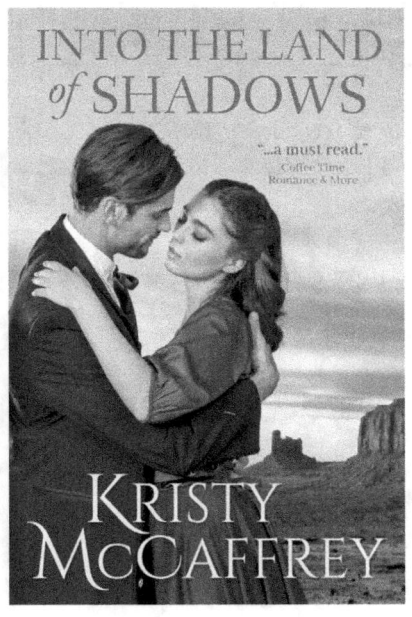

A Stand-Alone Novel

This book was previously published in 2013 under the same title. While the text and cover have been updated, the story remains the same.

It's been five years since a woman came between Ethan Barstow and his brother, Charley, and it's high time they buried the hatchet. When Ethan travels to Arizona Territory to make amends, he learns that Charley has abruptly disappeared after breaking more than one heart in town. And an indignant fiancée is hot on his trail.

When Charley Barstow abandons a local girl after getting her pregnant, Kate Kinsella pursues him without a second thought. She's determined he set things right, and even more determined to end her own engagement to him, a sham from the beginning. But an ill-timed encounter with a group of ruffians lands her in the company of Charley's brother, Ethan, who suggests they search together.

As Ethan and Kate move deeper INTO THE LAND OF SHADOWS, family tensions and past tragedies threaten to destroy a love neither of them expected.

kmccaffrey.com/into-the-land-of-shadows/

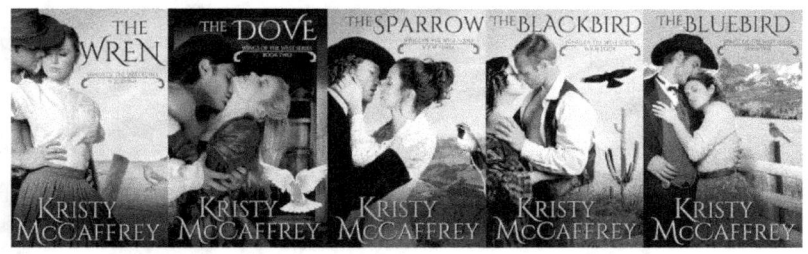

Don't miss the Wings of the West series

Honorable men and courageous women. Experience the grit, the hope, and the romance of the Old West.

"Ms. McCaffrey writes from the heart…" ~ The Romance Studio

THE WREN – Captured by Comanche as a child, Molly Hart was assumed dead. Ten years later, Texas Ranger Matt Ryan finds a woman with the same blue eyes.

THE DOVE – Reunited with Logan Ryan on the steps of the White Dove Saloon, Claire Waters hides under the guise of a fancy girl…and lets the ex-deputy believe the worst.

THE SPARROW – Within Grand Canyon, raging rapids and ancient spirits sweep Texas Ranger Nathan Blackmore and Emma Hart into a wild adventure.

THE BLACKBIRD – Haunted by a deadly attack, Tess Carlisle turns to bounty hunter Cale Walker to find her missing *padre*. But in the land of the Apache, can he free her heart?

THE BLUEBIRD – Molly Rose Simms arrives in Colorado to meet her brother, but instead finds herself searching for the mythical Bluebird mining claim with a man known as The Jackal.

Learn more about each book at Kristy's website
kmccaffrey.com/books/

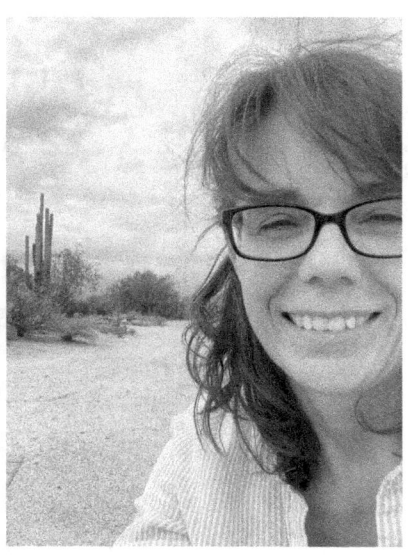

Kristy McCaffrey has been writing since she was very young, but it wasn't until she was a stay-at-home mom that she considered becoming published. A fascination with science led her to earn two mechanical engineering degrees—she did her undergraduate work at Arizona State University and her graduate studies at the University of Pittsburgh—but storytelling has always been her passion. She writes both contemporary tales and award-winning historical western romances.

An Arizona native, Kristy and her husband reside in the desert where they frequently remove (rescue) rattlesnakes from their property and try to coax their American bulldog, Jeb, to go for walks (he's moody and lazy). She also spends her time reading and researching her next book and playing with her three grandchildren.

"The world is full of magic things, patiently waiting for our senses to grow sharper." ~ W.B. Yeats

Connect with Kristy
    Website: kmccaffrey.com

Newsletter: kmccaffrey.com / subscribe
Facebook: facebook.com / AuthorKristyMcCaffrey
Instagram: instagram.com / kristymccaffreybooks
BookBub: bookbub.com / authors / kristy-mccaffrey
TikTok: tiktok.com / @kristymccaffrey

www.ingramcontent.com/pod-product-compliance
Lightning Source LLC
Chambersburg PA
CBHW061204170626
46809CB00003B/1237